What's the Difference?

Also from **mental**_floss:

mental_floss *presents: Condensed Knowledge*

mental_floss *presents: Forbidden Knowledge*

mental_floss *presents: Instant Knowledge*

mental_floss: *Cocktail Party Cheat Sheets*

mental_floss: *Scatterbrained*

mental_floss: *The Genius Instruction Manual*

mental_floss

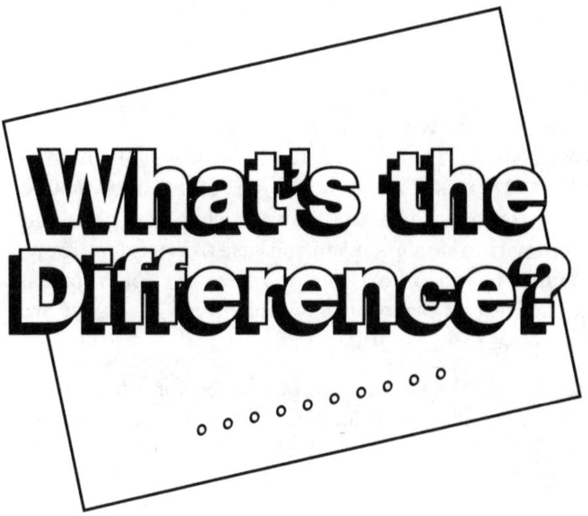

Edited *by* Will Pearson, Mangesh Hattikudur, and John Green

Written *by* John Green, Maggie Koerth, Chris Connolly and Christopher Smith

An Imprint of HarperCollins*Publishers*

HarperCollins books may be purchased for educational, business, or sales promotional use. For information, please write: Special Markets Department, HarperCollins Publishers, 10 East 53rd Street, New York, NY 10022.

FIRST EDITION

Designed by Emily Cavett Taff
Illustrations by Stephen Smith

Library of Congress Cataloging-in-Publication Data has been applied for.

ISBN-10: 0-06-088249-2
ISBN-13: 978-0-06-088249-5

06 07 08 09 10 WB/RRD 10 9 8 7 6 5 4 3 2 1

Contents

Forewords vs. Prefaces vs. Introductions

o o o o o o o o o o o

The other day, our editor called us and said that we needed to write something called a "Preface" to this book, which begged in our hearts important questions: What is a preface? Isn't that just the same thing as a foreword? And also, is that something our intern could do or is it something we need to do ourselves?

As it turns out, *preface, foreword,* and *introduction* are not synonyms. To quote *The Chicago Manual of Style:* "A foreword is usually a statement by someone other than the author, sometimes an eminent person whose name can be carried on the title page." A preface, meanwhile, is written by the author, and often includes acknowledgments along with the reason that the person wrote the book. An introduction, unlike a preface or foreword, is required reading, because it is actually the beginning of the book's narrative (in nonfiction, this is often historical background).

Anyway, we figured we'd have all three.

The Foreword

Once in a great while, a book comes along that is not only funny and wise, but also genuinely important. Newton's *Principia Mathematica.* Or Darwin's *On the Origin of Species.* It is my great pleasure to announce that another such book has entered the world. *What's the Difference?* has taught me much that I did not previously know, like, for instance, the distinction between mayonnaise and Miracle Whip. Also, as I am Jewish, I never really understood the difference between a basilica and a cathedral. Now I do, and I am a better man for it. So thank you to the staff of ***mental**_floss*. As a token of my appreciation, I am sending them the medal awarded me by the Nobel committee in 1921.

Forever in your debt,
—Albert Einstein

The Preface

Now, we're not going to say that our book *What's the Difference?* has the power to heal the sick and raise the dead. All we're saying is that Albert Einstein wrote our foreword. The preface is where we discuss why we chose to write this particular book. Aside from our burning desire to have Mr. Einstein recognize our work, we wanted to bring light where there is darkness, to bring clarity where there is confusion, and also to figure out the difference between Monet and Manet. We, as it happens, are married to an art historian (which we guess means that either our wife is a bigamist or "we" are using the royal "we"), and so Impressionism comes up a fair bit in our household. Before this book, we would always pronounce a clear "muh" and a clear "nay" whenever talking about either artist, but then in the middle we just used some weird vowel that's halfway between *o* and *a* in the hopes that our wife wouldn't notice that we are a total idiot.

So obviously this is an important book to read if you happen to be married to an art historian. But it's also vital for many other people—for instance, those who may one day be attacked by huge furry creatures. With the help of this book, you'll quickly be able to establish whether your assailant is a black bear, a grizzly, or a reincarnated Andre the Giant. But even if this book never saves your life, we guarantee you'll feel smarter upon finishing it. (Note: That is *not* a money-back guarantee.)

—*The Intern*

The Introduction

This, according to our completely infallible *The Chicago Manual of Style,* is supposed to contain only "material essential to the text, material that should be read before the rest of the book," of which we have absolutely none. So you can just go ahead and turn the page now. Thanks, and enjoy.

Either nothing, or
—*John Green*

What's the Difference?

Aa Bb Cc Dd Ee
Jj Kk Ll Mm Nn
Ss Tt Uu Vv

English

○ ○ ○ ○ ○ ○ ○ ○ ○ ○

Idiot vs. Moron

The Dilemma: You want to assail someone's intelligence, but you don't know quite which word to use, which calls into question your own intellect.

People You Can Impress: Well, idiots and morons both, for starters. But also psychologists. And you really, really need to impress psychologists, because—as you'll see—you don't want them to think you're an idiot.

The Quick Trick: These days, the words are completely synonymous. But back in the dark days of psychology (which is to say until about 30 years ago), there was a difference, and here's the quick trick psychologists used: Ask a question. If your subject answers, they're a moron at worst. If they don't answer, you might have an idiot on your hands.

The Explanation:

Anyone who says that political correctness never accomplished anything worthwhile should take a long, hard look at the lot of the idiot.

In 1911, French psychologists Alfred Binet and Theodore Simon created the first modern intelligence test, which measured intelligence (hence the "intelligence quotient") based on whether children could accomplish tasks like pointing to their nose (honestly) and counting pennies. The concept of "IQ" followed soon after, and psychologists fell so deeply in love with the scientific nature of the tests that they created classification systems. Any child with an IQ of above 70 was considered "normal," while those with scores above 130 were considered "gifted." To classify scores *below* 70, psychologists invented a nomenclature of retardation. Those with IQs between 51 and 70 were called *morons*. Morons had adequate learning skills to complete menial tasks and communicate. *Imbeciles*, with IQs between 26 and 50, never progressed past a mental age of about six. And the lowest of all were the *idiots*, with IQs between 0 and 25, who were characterized by poor motor skills, extremely limited communication, and little response to stimulus.

The moron/imbecile/idiot classifications remained popular, amazingly, until the early 1970s, when people started to note that the developmentally disabled have enough difficulties without being saddled with condescending labels.

Today the classification system is one category broader—*moron, imbecile,* and *idiot* have been replaced with *mild, moderate, severe,* and *profound retardation*—and diagnostic factors other than IQ are considered in making a diagnosis.

Good to Know

The doubly offensive term "Mongolian idiot," which in the 19th and early 20th centuries was an actual, literal diagnosis, derives from people's belief that individuals with Down syndrome—with their wide-set eyes and round faces—resembled Mongolians. In fact, before the British physician J.H.L. Down (1828–1896) lent his name to the chromosomal syndrome, Down syndrome was known merely as "mongolism."

o o o o o o o o o o

I.e. vs. E.g.

The Dilemma: You're reading a document that's riddled with needless, pretentious Latin abbreviations (a legal brief, e.g., or ***mental_****floss*'s exploration of differences—i.e., this book), but your year of high school Latin has been obscured by the fog of memory.

People You Can Impress: Roman emperors, lawyers, and grammar nerds

The Quick Trick: *E.g.* means "for example"; *i.e.* means "that is." We at ***mental_****floss* remember this simply by employing Valley Girl speak. Where a fancypants Latinist would use e.g., a Valley Girl would use "like." And where the Latinist uses *i.e.*, the Valley girl goes with "I mean." Like: "I love going out with Todd. He has, like, a really nice car. I mean, it cost a lot of money."

The Explanation:

We will never understand why English abbreviations like BRB and LOL are derided as lazy, while Latin abbreviations are seen as the height of class. But now and again, it just *sounds* better to spice things up with a little dead language, and since Greek and Sanskrit both use unfamiliar alphabets, Latin's your best bet.

E.g. is short for *exempli gratia*, which literally means "by grace of example." *I.e.* is more straightforward: *id est* means "that is." The confusion stems from the fact that both abbreviations seek to clarify or focus a broad proposition, but *e.g.* is followed by a specific example, whereas *i.e.* is followed by a restatement.

Now that you know your *i.e.* from your *e.g.*, we hereby provide a guide to other Latin abbreviations and phrases that some people use, even though the English language has already stolen all the Latin words it needs.

Other Helpful Latin Abbreviations

C.f.: Often misused to mean "see, for instance," c.f. is actually short for *confer*. *Confer* is the imperative of *conferre* and means "compare" in Latin even though it means no such thing in English. Just remember c.f. should be used in English only to mean "compare with."

Etc.: Literally, "and the rest," *etc.* (the abbreviation of *etcetera*) indicates that the list it follows is partial. For that reason, it's redundant, and therefore poor grammar, to say, "I love hair metal; e.g., Whitesnake, Poison, Damn Yankees, etc.," since the "for example" immediately makes it clear that the list is partial.

QED: An abbreviation for *quod erat demonstradum* that means "which was to be demonstrated." These days, QED generally means "Look, Mom, I proved it!" Mathematicians sometimes still end their proofs with "QED," and you sometimes hear lawyers say it, because lawyers will say absolutely anything in Latin.

○ ○ ○ ○ ○ ○ ○ ○ ○ ○ ○

En Dash vs. Em Dash

The Dilemma: You're writing an important memo/term paper/***mental_floss*** book, and you need a dash. But not just any dash.

People You Can Impress: almost no one, really

The Quick Trick: It's almost always an em dash. No document can ever contain too many em dashes—in this book alone we use 173.

The Explanation:

Having learned to not dangle your participles or split your infinitives,* grammar offers bolder, deeper mysteries. Like, can you start a sentence with *like*? And what about starting (or finishing) a sentence with *and*? And also, what's the difference between an en dash and an em dash? The answers to those questions: Sure; yeah; and well, read on.

An en dash (–) is bigger than a hyphen but shorter than an em dash (—). The names come from an obscure typographical measurement system, but the dashes have now taken on a life of their own in grammar. The em dash is the spork of English grammar: It ain't particularly pretty, but you can use it for most anything. Em dashes can replace colons or sets of parentheses, or represent a sudden change in thought or tone.

But if the em dash is a spork, then the en dash is nothing less than a salad fork: We often forget what it looks like and when to use it. But here are the two basic uses of en dashes:

* Both of which, you will no doubt note, we did in that very sentence.

1. To show numerical ranges, signifying "up to and including"—of dates, ages, pages, etc. (Example: "I read pages 7–22 last night.")
2. The storied "compound adjective hyphen," an event so rare in the English language that proofreaders shiver with excitement whenever they come across it. Basically "pro-American" gets a regular hyphen because "American" is only one word, whereas "pro–Falkland Islands" gets an en dash because "Falkland Islands" is two words. So, too phrases like "Civil War–era."

The Grammar Roundup

Colon vs. Semicolon: Semicolons connect two complete sentences; colons start lists, introduce quotations, and extract water from feces. Oh, wait. Different colon.

Slash vs. Backslash: The backslash was invented in 1960 and is used almost exclusively in computing; the forward slash was invented by the ancient Romans and is often used in place of a hyphen.

What the ‽

The newest punctuation mark, by far, is the interrobang, which has the kind of name you just want to keep repeating. An exclamation point superimposed on a question mark, the interrobang is for those questions that are also exclamations, like: "Arnold Schwarzenegger is *pregnant*‽" Invented by advertising executive Martin K. Speckter in 1962, the interrobang became a key on some typewriters and was featured in newspapers. But alas, its popularity waned. Today you have to scroll all the way down your font list to Wingdings 2 to find the interrobang on Windows-based computers.

o o o o o o o o o o

Charlie Sheen vs. Emilio Estevez

The Dilemma: You've just finished a brilliant, heartbreaking screenplay titled *Mighty Ducks 5*. But you can't remember whether to slip it under Sheen or Estevez's door.

People You Can Impress: rabid *Men at Work* fans

The Quick Trick: You saw Estevez in *The Breakfast Club*; Sheen in *Wall Street*. (So to answer your dilemma: It's Estevez.)

The Explanation:

SHEEN

5'10"

Born Carlos Estevez (took his father's stage name to ride his coattails)

Divorced from a quasi-celebrity (he was married to Denise Richards from 2002 to 2005)

Has often been forced to talk about his romantic relationships in court (he once accidentally shot then-girlfriend Kelly Preston, was twice charged with beating women, and admitted paying $50,000 for prostitutes during the trial of Hollywood madam Heidi Fleiss).

Best movies: *Platoon, Wall Street, Major League*

Worst movies: *Grizzly II: The Predator, All Dogs Go to Heaven 2*—there have been a lot, really.

ESTEVEZ

5'7"

Born Emilio Estevez (refused to take his father's stage name because he didn't want to ride his coattails)

Divorced from a quasi-celebrity (he was married to Paula Abdul from 1992 to 1994)

Never talks about his romantic relationships

Best movies: *The Breakfast Club, St. Elmo's Fire, The War at Home*

Worst movies: The latter two-thirds of the *Mighty Ducks* franchise certainly didn't get a lot of Oscar buzz.

The Sheens: A Family Circle

-Joe Estevez (appeared in more than 125 movies, like *Max Hell Comes to Frogtown* [2002]) BROTHER TO →

- Martin Sheen (*West Wing, Wall Street,* etc.) FATHER TO →

-Renée Estevez (bit parts in everything from *The War at Home* to Red *Shoe Diaries* 5) SISTER TO →

-Charlie Sheen (already discussed) FATHER TO →

-Sam Sheen (In a record even for Sheen/Estevezes, Sam was born on March 9, 2004, and got her first acting gig just eight months later, playing a baby on Sheen's show *Two and a Half Men.*) NIECE TO →

-Ramon Estevez (a bit part in *Alligator 2: The Mutation* might be the highlight of his career) BROTHER TO →

-Emilio Estevez (already discussed) FATHER TO →

-Taylor Estevez (bit parts in two movies, both of which starred his father) BROTHER TO →

-Paloma Estevez (bit part in one movie, *The War at Home,* which starred her father *and* grandfather)

o o o o o o o o o o o

Polytheism vs. Pantheism

The Dilemma: You're chatting with a cute girl at a party, and she calls herself a pantheist. You want to ask a good follow-up question, but your limited knowledge of Greek prefixes has gotten you all flustered.

People You Can Impress: Pagans, wiccans, Hindus, Buddhists—pretty much everyone except Christians, Jews, and Muslims

The Quick Trick: *Poly* means "many"; *pan* means "all." So if you're looking to worship a bunch of things, go with polytheism. If you want to worship *everything,* go with pantheism.

The Explanation:

Very simply, polytheism is the belief in multiple deities, and pantheism is the belief that God is everything and everything is God. While the polytheist may believe in Zeus *and* Hera, the pantheist probably believes in Zeus and Hera and every other deity as part of the primary force in all things.

But the simplicity of this difference masks a world of confusion. Take Hinduism, which is usually considered to be a polytheistic religion because it contains enough gods to pack the Rose Bowl. However, many Hindus are not polytheistic. They view all gods as manifestations or aspects of the one Supreme God, which is every bit as monotheistic as the Christian belief in the Trinity. However, some Hindus are pantheistic, believing that just as all the various gods are aspects of the one true God, so is everything else in creation. Wait. So who's on first? (Aside from Vishnu, Ganesha, Shiva, Brahma, and Lakshmi.)

In reality, the problem stems from a desire to boil down religious traditions into something simpler than they are. It's true, for instance, that most Buddhists don't believe in any gods, ergo no word with *theist* in it applies to them, but the Buddhist belief that everything in the cosmos has "universal Buddha nature" is *sorta* pantheistic. Accusations of pantheism are frequently leveled against mystical sects of monotheistic religions, like Kabbalah in Judaism, Sufism in Islam, and Gnosticism in Christianity.

All in all, you're well advised never to label a people pantheistic *or* polytheistic unless they identify themselves as such. Although both words have clear meanings, the actual application of them exposes the diversity within all religious traditions.

Polyamory vs. Polygamy

Polyamory means that you're part of a long-term sexual relationship that involves more than two people; *polygamy* means you've made it official with a wedding. (Or multiple weddings, actually.) Polyamory is legal in the United States, and, in fact, its proponents claim there are thousands of happily polyamorous Americans. Polygamy is illegal, although prosecutions are rare.

Polygamy itself comes in two *poly-* varieties: *Polygyny* means having more than one wife or female mate at a time and is also the shortest word in the English language containing three *y*'s. *Polyandry* means having more than one husband or male mate at a time.

Sure, but is there such a thing as *panamory,* for those of us who literally want to do it with *everything?* Not yet, but be patient. *Polyamory* didn't become a popular word until 1990; *panamory* can't be far behind.

o o o o o o o o o o

Disciples vs. Apostles

The Dilemma: You're vaguely worried about a pop quiz at the Pearly Gates.

People You Can Impress: well, Jesus, obviously

The Quick Trick: Unless Jesus Christ himself has named you an apostle, discipleship is really the best you can hope for.

The Explanation:

The words are often used interchangeably, but they don't quite share a meaning. All Christians are (or at least ought to be) disciples of Christ, because they follow his teachings. (*Disciple* comes from the Latin *discipulus,* which means "pupil.") But very, very few Christians have ever been full-on apostles, because "apostle" is a title that only Jesus himself could give someone. If a disciple is a pupil, then an apostle is something of a traveling salesman (its Greek root word technically means "delegate," but "traveling salesman" is funnier). The 12 disciples officially became Jesus' delegates when he personally sent them out into the world to preach and heal.

Over the years, many people have claimed that Jesus named them apostles (see, for instance, David Koresh), and many evangelical Christian groups believe that *all* their members are apostles who've been dispatched by Jesus—which is why they often show up on your doorstep. But all Christians agree that there have been at least 13 apostles: the 12 ODs (that is, Original Disciples) and the apostle Paul, who met Jesus after his resurrection.

The 12: A Quick Rundown

Simon called Peter: Fisherman who left his nets to follow Jesus; became the first pope; probably crucified around 64 CE.

Andrew: Peter's brother; didn't get to be pope, but probably did get crucified (on an X-shaped cross, now known as a St. Andrew's Cross and seen on the flag of Scotland).

James: Known as "St. James the Greater"; one of the first to follow Jesus; wasn't crucified, but was martyred by the sword.

John: Possibly the author of The Gospel According to John and The Book of Revelation to John; he was the rare disciple who lived to old age.

Philip: Not widely mentioned in the Gospels, Philip reportedly died during a crucifixion even though a miraculous earthquake shook him loose from the cross.

Bartholomew: Pals with Philip, Bartholomew (according to tradition) was flayed alive in Armenia and then crucified upside down.

Matthew: Known as "the tax collector" and the author of The Gospel According to Matthew, tradition holds that Matthew was martyred in either Ethiopia or Parthia.

Thomas: The Thomas behind "Doubting Thomas," he is supposed to have been the first missionary to India. Martyred, naturally.

James: Known by the unfortunate moniker "James the Lesser" and barely mentioned in the gospels, although he may have written the underread Book of James. Probably martyred.

Simon: Commonly referred to as "Simon the Zealot," he was reportedly put to death by a saw.

Judas Iscariot: Most likely betrayed Jesus for 30 lousy pieces of silver, and ended up killing himself.

The Other Judas: So many people got Judas Thaddeus confused with the-Judas-who-betrayed-Jesus that veneration of Thaddeus came to be known as a "lost cause." Thaddeus is now the patron saint of lost causes. Martyred.

Pluto vs. Goofy

The Dilemma: They're both dogs, right? And they're both Disney characters. So why's one of them walking around on two legs and chatting up a storm while the other's resigned to barking on all fours and lapping from a water bowl?

People You Can Impress: Mickey, Minnie, Scrooge McDuck, Dumbo, Darkwing Duck, Lady, the Tramp, Chip, Dale, and Baloo Bear from *TaleSpin**

The Quick Trick: Goofy talks; Pluto doesn't.

The Explanation:

To begin with, cartoon dogs are generally not known as "dogs" but as "dawgs." Believe it or not, this convention dates all the way back to the 1920s. So neither Goofy nor Pluto is a dog; they are both dawgs. Pluto, however, is a *pet,* whereas Goofy is equal to (albeit stupider than) the other anthropomorphized residents of the Disney universe.

A character similar to Pluto first appeared in 1930 as a bloodhound named Rover. Rover quickly became Minnie Mouse's pet dog, and then Disney changed his name to Pluto and made Mickey Mouse the owner. Over the years, the versatile Pluto has also played Donald Duck's pet dog. In fact, Pluto

* Note: Several years ago, our friend Hank bet us that we could never get "Baloo Bear" into a book. Checkmate, sir. That will be five American dollars.

was among the most popular Disney characters in the '30s and '40s, often appearing in his own cartoons opposite such friends as Dinah the Dachshund and such enemies as Chip 'n' Dale, who went on to have their own success as Rescue Rangers.

But Pluto has fallen out of favor lately: He was the only major character *not* featured in 1984's *Mickey's Christmas Carol.* Goofy, whose full name is Goofy Goof, has fared far better, perhaps because kids prefer their dawgs talking. Goofy debuted in 1932, and was known variously as Dippy Dawg (see?!), Mr. Geef, and Dippy the Goof before his name was solidified in 1934. The highlight of Goofy's early career was 1951's *No Smoking,* in which he fights a nicotine craving to hilarious effect. Goofy's star faded for decades: Between 1961 and the mid-1990s, the professional doofus nearly disappeared from the Disney pantheon. But what a comeback he's made. After the success of his TV show *Goof Troop,* Goofy has become a star in many of Disney's direct-to-DVD animations, including 2000's *An Extremely Goofy Movie,* which we regret to report is also An Extremely Cloying Movie. Pluto should be so lucky as to have the comeback his chatty, pants-wearing pal has enjoyed.

Pluto vs. Other Tiny Planets

Some astronomers argue that a celestial object, currently known by the catchy name 2003UB313, is more of a planet than Pluto is—and that *it* either should be the ninth planet or kids should have to memorize a tenth planet name. That said, it's definitely going to mess up a lot of mnemonic devices: "My Very Earnest Mother Just Served Us Nine Pickles 2003UB313" just doesn't roll off the tongue.

o o o o o o o o o o

Paul vs. Saul

The Dilemma: You've read his writing, or at the very least heard his First Letter to the Corinthians at 100,000 weddings ("Love is not boastful," etc.). But what's the real name of the 13th apostle?

People You Can Impress: biblical scholars and people named Paul (also, people named Saul, although a lot of them tend to be either elderly or dead)

The Quick Trick: Before he saw Jesus, he was Saul; thereafter, Paul.

The Explanation:

Just as Prince became the Artist Formerly Known as Prince, Saul of Tarsus saw fit to have a midcareer name change. But Saul's transformation was even more radical than Prince's: Saul was a Jewish tentmaker who may have possessed Roman citizenship and persecuted Christians; Paul was a Christian—in fact, he was probably the single most important person in Christian history not named Jesus.

The change came about while Saul was on the road to Damascus around 35 CE, when Jesus appeared before him in a vision. Called by Christ to apostleship, Saul became Paul, and Paul quickly became one of the most important leaders of the young church. As a Jew, Paul was able to ground his theology in the Judaism of Jesus and most of the fledgling band of Christians. But Paul saw his true mission as being "the apostle to the gentiles," and with his knowledge of Roman traditions, he was well placed to preach to non-Jewish residents of the empire. In his letters to various congregations, many of which ended up in the New Testament, Paul's emphasis on the mystical importance of the resurrection of Christ, along with his exhortations to evangelize to the gentiles, helped establish Christianity as we know it today, as a religion entirely separate from Judaism. Paul also founded churches in Asia Minor and possibly even Spain and Britain.

Although little is known for certain about his life after the letters in the New Testament (most of which date to the 50s CE, making them some of the New Testament's earliest writings), Paul is believed to have been—you'll never believe it—martyred around 67 CE.

John vs. John vs. John vs. John

A BRIEF GUIDE TO THE BIBLICAL JOHNS

John the Baptist: A prophet to Christians and Muslims alike, J the B was a radical, locust-eating preacher who baptized folks in the desert. When Jesus visited John, he hailed Jesus as the Second Coming. Unfortunately, he was beheaded on orders from Herod.

John the Apostle: One of the 12 apostles. Possibly the author of the Gospel According to John; possibly the author of the epistles of John; and possibly the author of Revelation. But probably none of the above, since all those works date to the late first century/early second century.

John the Evangelist: The name used to refer to the author of The Gospel According to John, whoever he was.

John of Patmos: The name used to refer to the author of Revelation, whoever he was.

o o o o o o o o o o o

Tom Sawyer vs. Huck Finn

The Dilemma: You know one of these rascals is the star of the Great American Novel, but which one?

People You Can Impress: the Widow Douglas, Aunt Polly, Injun Joe, Jim—and most important, noted hottie Becky Thatcher

The Quick Trick: *Huck Finn* is brilliant; *Tom Sawyer* isn't.

The Explanation:

Mark Twain's *Adventures of Huckleberry Finn* (1885) was among the first American novels written in the vernacular. Twain always felt strongly that writing ought to reflect the way people talk (for a hilarious meditation on the topic, see Twain's "Fenimore Cooper's Literary Offenses," in which Twain takes Cooper and, to use the vernacular of *our* day, tears him a new one). *Huckleberry Finn* was by far the greatest book Twain ever wrote. Set before the Civil War, it tells the story of one Huck Finn, the son of a violent drunk. Huck's dad kidnaps him from his civilized foster home. Huck escapes his dad and ends up floating on a raft with a slave named Jim who is seeking freedom in the North. Although Huck's conscience tells him he ought to do the legal thing and turn Jim in, he just can't bring himself to do it. The conflict between Huck's "deformed conscience," as Twain called it, and his personal feelings is what makes Huck such an extraordinary hero. And Jim, whose dialect is brilliantly rendered, emerges as, to quote the novelist Russell Baker, the book's "only true gentleman." It's a staggering inversion of 19th-century expectations: Doing the right thing means going against your conscience, and sometimes the noblest man in a story is black. Plus *Huck Finn* is a wonderful adventure story, which is why it was initially published not for adults but kids. Adults, as it happened, ended up loving it, too. Ernest Hemingway once wrote, "All modern American literature comes from one book by Mark Twain called *Huckleberry Finn*. . . . It's the best book we've had."

You're not likely to catch anyone calling *The Adventures of Tom Sawyer* "the best book we've had." *Tom Sawyer* is about the rollicking life of boys in a riverside town—and it ain't much deeper than that. Tom convinces other children to whitewash a fence for him; Tom and Huck explore Injun Joe's cave; Tom and Huck try their best to win the affection of pigtailed blonde Becky Thatcher, etc. Critics view *Tom Sawyer* as little more than a well-written, nostalgic romp through Twain's childhood in Hannibal, Missouri. It's plenty of fun, but Tom's simpleminded mischievousness just can't match Huck's thoughtfulness and despite-his-best-efforts heroism.

Banning Books

When the American Library Association compiled a list of the books people most frequently attempt to ban from schools and libraries during the 1990s, *Huck Finn* came in fifth. (It was beat by, among others, the filthy, profanity-ridden, borderline-pornographic drivel known as—well—*Harry Potter and the Chamber of Secrets*.)

o o o o o o o o o o

Geek vs. Nerd vs. Dork

The Dilemma: You're proud to be all three of these supposed insults! But you're wondering if one captures your brilliant essence better than the others.

People You Can Impress: well, not cool kids, certainly. Face it—we're never going to impress those jerks.

The Quick Trick: Etymologically, *geek* probably equals *carny, nerd* probably equals *Seussian animal,* and *dork* probably equals what you might have called President Nixon if you were his close friend.

The Explanation:

All three of these words are now used interchangeably to refer to someone who is undesirable due to a paucity of social skills and an excess of braininess. Fortunately, former middle-school punching bags have co-opted all three words, turning them from insults into badges of honor. But while the words have come to overlap in meaning, their etymologies couldn't be more different. So for all those of us who've suffered such verbal barbs—and what proud ***mental_floss*** reader hasn't?—here's what they were *really* saying about you.

GEEK

Etymological Theory 1: Sometime in the early 19th century, the Scottish word *geck,* meaning "fool," changed to *geek* and began being used to describe a certain kind of carnival performer. Geeks specialized in eating live animals, including biting the heads off live chickens.

Theory 2: Real etymology geeks trace the word *geck* all the way back to Shakespeare—see, for instance, "the most notorious geck" in Act V of *Twelfth Night*—and claim that we have the first great literature geek to blame for the word.

NERD

Theory 1: The first known appearance of the word is in Dr. Seuss's 1950 *If I Ran the Zoo*, in which a character wants to collect "A Nerkle a Nerd and a Seersucker, too!" The theory goes that kids liked the ring of the word so much, they started using it derogatorily.

Theory 2: Some at Rensselaer Polytechnic Institute claim that they coined the word *knurd* in the '50s to describe kids who studied all the time (*knurd* being *drunk* spelled backward).

DORK

This time, there's only one theory: The word *dork* originally meant "penis." (Specifically, human penis.) Popularized in the '60s, *dork* was probably derived from *dirk*, a penile name that was widely used until the short version of Richard became ubiquitous.

Old School Nerds

Before the words *nerd* and *dork* existed, there were still nerds and dorks. According to *Dewdroppers, Waldos, and Slackers*, a guide to 20th-century American slang, all these words have been used to describe the unpopular, undesirable, and generally square: *wind sucker, dewdropper, Joe Zilch, dudd, pantywaist, oil can, stinkeroo, mullet, nosebleed, roach, schnookle, kook, dimp, dorf, mince, squid, auger,* and *waldo.*

o o o o o o o o o o

The Iliad vs. The Odyssey

The Dilemma: You read these two epic poems in college for class. Or, more precisely, you scanned them. Well, you never technically cracked the spine of either book, and now you can't spot a Cyclops from a Trojan Horse. Help!

People You Can Impress: potentially, Brad Pitt. Also anyone who loves the phrase "It's all Greek to me."

The Quick Trick: If it's happening on a boat, it's *The Odyssey*; if it's not, it's probably *The Iliad*. Also, *The Iliad* stars Achilles; *The Odyssey*, Odysseus.

The Explanation:

Both of these epic poems are attributed to Homer, the Greek poet who may or may not have ever existed (if he did, it may have been in the eighth century BCE). *The Iliad* tells the story of the so-called Trojan War, a war that may or may not have actually happened due to a boy, Menelaus, and another boy, Paris, being in love with the same girl, Helen. As the story goes, it was out of this love triangle that the fierce battle between the Greeks and the Trojans was born.

As for *The Iliad* itself, it focuses on the 10th and final year of the war. Greek Achilles (today known primarily as a heel and a tendon) is so angry with his commander-in-chief, Agamemnon, that he ceases fighting. The Trojan Hector, meanwhile, is a loyal soldier. Eventually, Achilles returns to battle and ends up (spoiler alert!) killing Hector. Upon seeing Hector's body, Achilles feels tremendous pity for the man, and the reader is made to understand the horrors of war.

The Iliad includes some of the oldest lyric poetry in the world, but it doesn't include the two most famous scenes from the Trojan War: the Trojan Horse and Achilles' death. Indeed, *The Iliad* hones in narrowly on Achilles' wrath and the tragic consequences of battle—making it, perhaps, the world's first antiwar poem.

While the story revolves mainly around Achilles, a fellow named Odysseus (or, as he was known to Romans and James Joyce, Ulysses) has a nice supporting role. Although Odysseus isn't central to *The Iliad,* he's an important part of stories about the war (for one thing, he came up with the whole idea of the Trojan Horse). But Odysseus' real moment in the spotlight comes *after* the war, in the 11,300-line story of his rambling, 10-year-long boat trip home known as *The Odyssey.*

The Odyssey also tells the story of Penelope, Odysseus' wife, who stands by her man despite having a roomful of suitors who insist he has died at sea. But the focus of the story is the heroic journey of Odysseus. He gets seduced by Sirens, his fellow travelers get turned into swine, and he defeats a Cyclops—all in the space of a few hundred pages. It is this epic that really forms a cornerstone of Western literature. From Virgil's *Aeneid* to the movie *O Brother, Where Art Thou?* countless works of art have been inspired by *The Odyssey.*

o o o o o o o o o o o

Socrates vs. Plato vs. Aristotle

The Dilemma: If you've seen one smart old Greek guy in a bedsheet, you've seen 'em all.
People You Can Impress: philosophy majors, Greeks, and any lingering fans of *Bill & Ted's Excellent Adventure*
The Quick Trick: It's simple! Just think of them in reverse alphabetical order: Socrates taught Plato who taught Aristotle who taught Alexander the Great.

The Explanation:

Like many a good philosopher, Socrates (470–399 or so BCE) was obsessed with truth and the correct way to stumble into it. In fact, in his effort to find truth, Socrates placed value not just on knowledge, but on how we *know* knowledge, and his inquisitive teaching style reflected it. For one thing, Socrates never lectured. Instead, he asked questions on top of questions (a teaching method still used to this day). The more his students answered, the more they knew or, more accurately, learned what they didn't know. For example, when you ask yourself, "Do I hate my job because I'm awful at it, or am I awful at my job because I hate it?" you're being Socratic in your search. As a master philosopher, Socrates' greatest rhetorical tool was irony, but not the *Seinfeld*-ian kind. Socratic irony is a tactic by which one pretends to be ignorant of another's dogmatic beliefs. And by asking apparently "innocent" questions, Socrates would then tear the other's position to ribbons.

Unfortunately for Socrates, endless questioning is also extremely annoying, and the barefoot philosopher's inquisitiveness made him powerful enemies. Put on trial for "corrupting the youth," Socrates was forced to commit suicide by drinking hemlock.

Luckily for us, his work lived on through his students. If Socrates wrote anything, it didn't survive. But his question-and-answer sessions were recorded by his pupils, Plato and Xenophon, in the dialogues. The former (427–347 BCE, give or take) also took it upon himself to expand on Socrates, and in the later dialogues Socrates is mostly AWOL, meaning it's all Plato. Plato's work didn't stop with the dialogues. His own writings dealt mostly with government, law, ethics, and reason. Today *The Republic* is considered Plato's major masterwork. In fact, his treatise on a "good city" is still a "must read" for poli-sci majors in universities everywhere.

Of these three philosophical bigwigs, however, it was Plato's student Aristotle (384–322 BCE) who had the most expansive intellect (not to mention the shortest beard). Aristotle wrote on literally every subject of the day, from metaphysics and government to mathematics and natural science. In fact, his renown as a polymath is what led Macedonian King Philip II (359–366 BCE) to choose Aristotle as a tutor for his son, Alexander. Aristotle departed from his two predecessors' line of thought, relying more on sensory input as a source of knowledge. Today Aristotle is thought of as the granddaddy of the scientific method—despite the fact that he relied on pure reason, not experiment, to come to a conclusion, and as a result was wrong a breathtakingly large percentage of the time.

Transsexual vs. Transvestite

The Dilemma: Oh, we bet you can imagine a few.
People You Can Impress: Mom and Dad, for sure
The Quick Trick: Transves*t*ites cross-dress (including, but not limited to, vests); transsexuals identify as members of the opposite sex.

The Explanation:

The word *transvestitism* was created by German psychologist Magnus Hirschfield around 1915 to describe people who cross-dress. But cross-dressing was around long before that. It's been common among eunuchs in India for centuries; in Norse mythology, famously masculine Thor once dressed like a woman; Shakespeare's characters did it in *Twelfth Night* and other plays; and so did 15th-century Pope Paul II. (Former FBI director J. Edgar Hoover, despite what you may have heard, probably did not cross-dress.) *Transvestitism* describes only the wearing of clothes—or accessories!—associated with another gender. In truth, cross-dressing has little to do with sexual preference, and experts estimate that only about 20 percent of cross-dressers are gay. Transsexualism, on the other hand, involves not wanting to *dress* as the other gender does, but wanting to be considered another gender. Transsexuals may or may not have undergone surgery and hormone therapy (after which they are often known as "post-op" to their friends) to complete their gender transformation, and while there are more male-to-female transsexuals, the number of female-to-male transsexuals seeking surgery and hormone treatment is growing.

Of course, all of this leads to some very sticky questions with regard to pronouns. Here's how it breaks down: Transvestites should be referred to by their genetic genders; i.e., someone born male who dresses in women's clothing is still a he. A genetic male *transsexual,* on the other hand, is a she, because she considers herself a woman and wishes to live as a woman in all ways, including the pronoun way.

(Inter)sexual Healing

Although most people have always thought of gender as being a one-or-the-other proposition, intersexuality proves that gender is a broad spectrum. Once known as hermaphrodites or pseudohermaphrodites, intersex people are born with gender-ambiguous genitalia. As many as 1 percent of all live births are intersex, usually resulting from a genetic mutation during fetal development. In fact, XX and XY are not the only possible gender chromosome combinations: There have been cases of XO, XXX, XXY, and XYY. Intersex children usually undergo surgery to help them conform to one gender or the other, but more and more, intersex rights groups are lobbying against such surgery, arguing that there's nothing wrong with being neither male nor female.

Who's Who

Eddie Izzard (British stand-up comedian): transvestite
Caroline Cossey ("Bond Girl" in 1981's *For Your Eyes Only*): transsexual
RuPaul: transvestite
Georgina Beyer (member of New Zealand's parliament): transsexual
Count Dracula: Transylvanian

o o o o o o o o o o o

Freud vs. Jung

The Dilemma: You dreamt about riding a horse bareback with your high school wrestling coach. Oh, and you were smoking a cigar. Should you be worried?

People You Can Impress: everyone at Group!

The Quick Trick: The id, ego, superego, and Oedipus stuff are Freudian; archetypes, extro- and introversion, and the collective unconscious are Jungian.

The Explanation:

Both Sigmund Freud (1856–1939) and Carl Jung (1875–1961) were so influential that they have become adjectives. But their story begins with Freud. Young Sigmund was the first one to push the idea of the unconscious (a.k.a. the part of your thought process that happens without you knowing it) on the masses. Freud thought that the best window into the unconscious was the dream, and he fixated on sexual development and the libido. In doing so, Freud divided childhood into the oral, anal, and phallic stages, based on what part of the body gives a child pleasure. It was here that he postulated his famous Oedipus complex—the one where sons want to kill Dad and marry Mom (the female version is the Elektra complex). It's no wonder, then, that Freud believed that a lot of humanity's problems came from repressed libidos. He thought, for instance, that women were particularly susceptible to "hysteria" (from the Greek for uterus, the same root as that of *hysterectomy*). And don't forget penis envy, his (now discredited) theory that women's psychological problems stemmed from their lack of said appendage.

Of course, Freud also brought words like *id, ego,* and *superego* into the popular lexicon. The id is home to our base instincts and desires, or our animal impulses; the superego is our subconscious nanny, keeping the id in check; and the ego is the I, balancing desire and acceptable behavior.

In addition, we still use lots of Freud's other terms in daily conversation, especially when psychoanalyzing our friends. Such coping mechanisms as projection (attributing our faults to others), denial (pretending something never happened), and rationalization (explaining something intellectually, removing the painful emotion) all come straight from Freud.

As for Carl Jung, Freud's slightly younger contemporary, he fathered analytic psychology. This was based on the idea that the conscious and unconscious minds need to be in harmony with each other. If not, you get *neuroses,* like depression or phobias.

We use a lot of Jungian gems, too. He coined the words *introvert* and *extrovert.* He also postulated the concept of the *collective* unconscious, or those shared mental characteristics that keep popping up in our cultures and dreams. Early in his career, Jung befriended Freud, but Jung quickly moved away from his predecessor's theories, emphasizing the role of myth, art, and religion in informing the unconscious.

My Coney Island Baby

Despite their differences, Freud and Jung once went to Coney Island together in 1909. Seriously. Our guess is that Jung found the Loop the Loop to be the archetypal roller coaster, while Freud probably found the whole place phallic and hysteria inducing.

o o o o o o o o o o

Purgatory vs. Limbo

The Dilemma: You're pretty sure that neither of these postmortem destinations is ideal—but if things don't work out as planned, you want to know which to pray for.

People You Can Impress: saints, sinners, and everyone in between

The Quick Trick: If you're reading this, you're probably not an infant—so purgatory's your main worry.

The Explanation:

Let's start with sin. Roman Catholics make a distinction based on a sin's severity. The biggies—murder, adultery, sacrilege, that type of thing—are called *mortal sins* because they put your soul in jeopardy of damnation. Die with one of those on your docket and you're pretty much screwed. The lesser sins that we all commit every day—petty jealousy, fibbing, cutting tags off of mattresses—well, those are *venial sins.* Confession and absolution free your soul from sin, but if you die with some venial demerits, you're off to Purgatory, table for one.

Contrary to some popular confusion, Purgatory is *not* the same thing as Hell. Not by a long shot. Purgatory is a place of punishment whereby your soul is cleansed. While theologians vary on the kind and severity of Purgatorial "punishment," some say that the agony of waiting for Heaven's rewards is punishment enough. Folks still living can pray for your soul to shorten your time there (November 2, All Soul's Day, is set aside specifically for this). Of course, once it's all shiny and sin free, your soul goes to Heaven to be in the presence of God, seeing God in a "beatific vision." Whereupon there is much rejoicing. Protestants reject Purgatory because it's not specifically in the Bible, among other reasons.

As for the doctrine of "limbo," it's so controversial that even Catholics aren't sure they believe in it. By definition, limbo is where the souls of those who are righteous or innocent, but not baptized (and therefore still stained by Adam's Original Sin), spend eternity deprived of joy. But there are actually two limbos. The first is *limbus patrum* (limbo of the fathers), where the souls of the just who predated Jesus Christ hung out until he freed us all from sin. The other, *limbus infantium,* is just what it sounds like—a home for the souls of babies who die before they can be baptized. It's a place of happiness, but free from the beatific vision, so ultimately a place of punishment for the sin of Adam (stupid fruit!). This doctrine is especially controversial within the Church, and some Catholics have begun accepting an alternative view—that the faithfulness of the parents can redeem an unbaptized baby's soul. An emotional issue, to say the least, making it a challenge to segue into the other limbo, but—well, we just did.

The Other Limbo

Trinidad's sacred ritual becomes a game 80-year-olds play on cruise ships. In the late 1950s, American tourists "borrowed" the limbo and turned it into a fixture at dinner parties, beach movies—even in rock-and-roll songs. In fact, Chubby Checker's "Limbo Rock" was the number 9 hit song of 1962.

Home
Ec

IZOD vs. Lacoste

The Dilemma: You want to look preppy. But how?
People You Can Impress: everyone at the country club, polo players, Republicans
The Quick Trick: Get a Lacoste shirt and you'll have the best of both worlds.

The Explanation:

As it turns out, Lacoste is a subbrand of IZOD. As Aristotle would put it: All Lacostes are IZODs, but not all IZODs are Lacostes. These days, both brands are owned by the garment giant Phillips-Van Heusen Corporation, so the difference between Lacoste IZODs and non-Lacoste IZODs is primarily marketing. But the difference between the men behind IZOD and Lacoste is vast indeed.

Jack Izod owned a tailoring shop in London, and billed himself as the "Shirtmaker to the King." Indeed, he made shirts for King George VI (1895–1951) in the 1930s. One day in the late '30s, a women's apparel magnate named Vin (no relationship to Diesel) Draddy visited IZOD's tailoring shop. Looking to start a line of men's clothing, Draddy recognized that his own last name would make a poor name for a clothing line, but he quite liked the ring of IZOD. So he bought the rights to IZOD's name and began making clothes under the IZOD moniker. Oddly enough, the brand's namesake, Jack Izod, never designed a single item for the company.

René Lacoste, on the other hand, really *did* design the

famous shirts named for him, which is all the more remarkable because he was not a tailor. He was a professional tennis player. Between 1925 and 1928, Lacoste won seven Grand Slam events, and might have won more had he not become ridiculously rich by inventing the world's first good tennis shirt. In the 1920s, tennis players wore long-sleeved, heavily starched dress shirts (often with ties!). Lacoste grew weary of the outfits, and by 1929, he'd designed a short-sleeved shirt with a longer shirttail in the back and a flat collar. Further proving he was ahead of his time, Lacoste generally played the game with his collar turned up, though it was more to block out the sun than anything else. But back to the shirts! Light and comfortable, Lacoste's garments were an immediate hit when he began mass-producing them in 1933. By 1951, he'd sold the brand to IZOD.

Lacoste's other significant contribution to fashion has to do with the iconic crocodile (it's not an alligator—see below) on his shirts. Known as "Le Crocodile" for his on-court tenacity, Lacoste added the crocodile to his shirts in the mid-1930s—the first time a logo is known to have appeared on the outside of a shirt. Not a bad fashion record for a guy who mostly just wanted to win tennis tournaments.

Alligator vs. Crocodile

So how can you tell the Lacoste symbol is a crocodile not an alligator? You can't, really, unless you know the story of Le Crocodile. But a *real* alligator and crocodile have many differences. For starters, crocodiles are much more likely to kill you. But also:

Crocodiles have a narrower, almost pointy snout.
A crocodile's lower teeth are always visible; an alligator's disappear when its mouth is closed.
Alligators are usually gray; crocodiles, a light brown.

o o o o o o o o o o

Egg Roll vs. Spring Roll

The Dilemma: You find yourself at a Chinese restaurant craving cylindrical food. But of which variety?

People You Can Impress: all the folks down at Hunan Garden. Now if you could only pronounce *Szechuan.*

The Quick Trick: If it's got a shell like a deep-fried tortilla, it's probably an egg roll. And if you're thinking that deep-frying tortillas is awfully American for Chinese food, you're onto something.

The Explanation:

The main gustatory difference between a spring roll and its egg cousin is that spring rolls have thin, often translucent flour wrappers, while egg rolls have thicker-wrappings (they are both fried, unlike their healthier cousin the summer roll). Also, spring rolls in America are often filled with carrots and bamboo, while egg rolls are more likely to be filled with meat and bean shoots. Oh, and one other difference: Spring rolls are Chinese; egg rolls probably aren't.

In fact, Chinese cuisine in America is so vastly different from Chinese cuisine in China that many American Chinese restaurants advertise, beneath their English names, "Westernized Food" in Chinese. In the 19th century, the primary audience for Chinese food was railroad workers, a group of people not widely known for their sophisticated palates. Chinese restaurateurs sought to accommodate both Chinese immigrants working the rails and their white coworkers—and in doing so created "fusion cuisine" long before it was hip. While some argue that egg rolls existed in China prior to their appearance in America, many food scholars believe that the egg roll is an American original. Besides the legendary roll, there are many staples of American Chinese food you'll rarely, if ever, see in China: fried rice, crab Rangoon, chow mein, sweet-and-sour pork, and General Tso's chicken. Also, fortune cookies (see below). What do all these foods have in common? Frying, which is a staple of American Chinese food but somewhat less important in authentic Chinese cuisine.

As for the spring roll, though, around the late 1980s, Americans began to turn against the very Chinese food they'd helped to invent. No longer could we afford to eat high-sodium foods sprinkled with MSG. And so more authentic Chinese restaurants started popping up, bringing back the relatively healthy spring roll. American Chinese cuisine still dominates the market in small towns, but the number of authentic restaurants grows every year.

How the Fortune Cookie Crumbles

Unlike the spring roll, the fortune cookie is not Chinese. It's actually *Japanese*-American. Makato Hagiwara, who designed (and for many years lived in) the Japanese Tea Garden in San Francisco's Golden Gate Park, invented the fortune cookie in the early 20th century. He intended the cookie to be a snack for people walking through the tea garden, but the concept became so popular that Chinese restaurants in San Francisco's Chinatown stole the idea.

o o o o o o o o o o

Paper vs. Plastic

The Dilemma: It happens every time you buy groceries. Your bagger casually asks, "Paper or plastic?" And if you don't answer within three seconds, people start looking at you funny. But it's a complex question requiring considerable analysis. Which is better for the environment? Easier to carry? Less likely to be a choking hazard? You could stand in that grocery line all day.

People You Can Impress: It's not about impressing anyone so much as not letting your indecisiveness aggravate the people in line behind you.

The Quick Trick: Plastic is probably better for the environment; paper is mostly better for the paper industry.

The Explanation:

First, let's dispense with the difference between paper and plastic bags. Most plastic bags are derived from crude oil or natural gas by-products that have been treated to form long chains of carbon and hydrogen molecules. They're then molded into the bag-with-handles shape we've known and loved at grocery stores since the mid-1980s. Paper bags, on the other hand, are made (you'll never believe it) from trees—specifically, compressed wood pulp.

So which is better? We'll begin with the case for plastic. For sheer ease of use, plastic certainly wins. Although the average paper grocery bag holds more than a plastic bag, plastic bags' handles make them much easier to carry. Also, plastic bags are cheaper (which is why when you respond to the paper-or-plastic question with an ambivalent shrug, baggers are usually taught to pick plastic). Plastic bags also take up less landfill space. According to one study (and yes, there are studies about this sort of thing) two plastic bags take up 72 percent less landfill space than one paper bag.

Proponents of paper are likely to point out that paper is easier to recycle, that plastic is derived from a nonrenewable resource, and that plastic is nonbiodegradable. But as it happens, paper isn't biodegradable either in modern American landfills, because landfills lack the water and soil needed for biodegrading. And it's true that paper is easier to recycle (although plastic bags *are* recyclable), but recycling itself takes energy and creates pollution.

All in all, every study we found agreed plastic was the better bag, requiring less total energy to create and producing less waste than paper. Of course, the *best* solution is to use neither paper nor plastic. Instead, you *could* bring your own reusable bags to the grocery store. But that seems like an *awful* lot of work just to slightly increase the chances that your children can live on a habitable planet.

The Ugly Factor

The movie *American Beauty* makes the flying plastic bag into a pretty metaphor, but most of us would agree that plastic bags floating through the air aren't so great. In South Africa, plastic bags came to be known as the "national flower" until 2004, when they were banned.

o o o o o o o o o o

Champagne vs. Sparkling Wine

The Dilemma: You're itching for a hangover, so you know bubbly booze is the way to go. But when you awake tomorrow in the cold gray light of the morning after, will one promise you a purer headache than the other?

People You Can Impress: everybody at the New Year's party. *Auld lang syne!* Whatever that means!*

The Quick Trick: This should be pretty easy to remember: *Champagne* is from Champagne; sparkling wine isn't.

The Explanation:

The French are really, really prickly about misuse of the word *champagne.* Only sparkling white wine that comes from the Champagne region of France, in the northeastern part of the country, can be called champagne. And that's not a suggestion; in Europe, it's the *law.* It has been illegal for non-Champaignois vineyards to call their booze champagne since 1891. In fact, so important is French ownership of the word *champagne* that it was reaffirmed in no less important a document than 1919's Treaty of Versailles—the one that ended World War I.

But here's the loophole: The United States never ratified the Treaty of Versailles—not because of the champagne clause, but because the Republican-controlled Congress didn't want to

* It literally means "old long ago" in old Scottish. Huh. Still don't get it.

see the formation of a League of Nations. And so, in America, it is perfectly legal to call your sparkling wine "champagne." In fact, you can call your gym shoes champagne, if you'd like. (What better way to exercise your freedom of speech!)

For decades, American producers of the bubbly called their products "champagne" left and right, but these days they tend to stick with "sparkling wine." Today many California producers tend to believe their products superior—mainly because California gets so much sunlight, and the richer grapes tend to produce drier wines. That may be true, but Cristal is still a heck of a lot better than Andre's pink champagne. True champagnes are usually aged longer than their American counterparts, and they're generally considered "more complex," which is sommelier-speak for "more expensive."

Dom Perignon

Although he did not invent champagne (it's been fermented in France since the Roman days), Benedictine monk Dom Pérignon (1638–1715) perfected it with improved fermentation and aging procedures. Upon first tasting his vastly improved champagne, Perignon is said to have exclaimed, "Come quickly, I am tasting the stars!" The champagne branded Dom Perignon, however, wasn't produced until 1936.

Bubbles (a.k.a. When Size Matters)

Conventional wisdom holds that the smaller the bubbles in sparkling wine, the better the booze. And it's true. Smaller bubbles mean more total bubbles, which help release the wine's flavor in the mouth. But bubble size is only one of many factors in determining champagne quality. The surest gauge? Price.

Counterfeit Bills vs. Real Money

The Dilemma: Someone just handed you a crisp $100 bill, and you're pretty sure the Franklin on there isn't supposed to be Aretha.

People You Can Impress: U.S. Treasury wonks and bank tellers

The Quick Trick: Spotting counterfeit bills is like discerning whether you're in love: If it feels real, it probably is.

The Explanation:

There are several strategies for spotting fake money. But for starters, try The Touch Test: Small-time thugs often forget that the paper U.S. money is printed on is a lot different from the stuff you put in your ink-jet printer. Instead of being made from tree-based cellulose, currency paper is made from cotton and linen fibers. You can easily feel the difference, so if counterfeiters want to be successful, they've got to make sure their money has the right touch. In 2002, Philadelphian Ricky Scott Nelson got around this quick trick by making his fake dollars out of real ones. He took actual $1 and $5 bills, used bleach to strip off the denomination markings and portraits, and photocopied them as $100 and $50 notes. Unfortunately for Nelson, his copying job still gave the bills away. The ink used on real money is never fully absorbed by the paper, leaving behind a distinct texture. Nelson's money, however, was smooth in all the wrong places.

If it feels real but you still aren't sure, it's time for Strategy 2: The Vending Machine Test: Unlike human cashiers, most vending machines can't tell a fake bill by touch or sight. So, in order to weed out the bad notes, they're programmed to check for magnetism. Fake bills don't have it. Real bills do because some of the ink the government uses for printing is magnetic.

If for some reason you're still convinced you've been passed a fake bill, try The Attention-to-Detail Test: If you turn a magnifying glass on a bill, you'll see that it contains intricate printing details not visible to the naked eye. For instance, the $20 bill is imprinted with a hexagonal pattern of lightly colored lines that give different parts of the bill different tints. Anything printed on an ink-jet printer would inevitably smudge those lines, turning the fake bill a brighter shade than that of a real one. Even a top-of-the-line printer will fudge some of the detail—if not these lines, then a bill's tiny dots and microprinted phrases—making it almost impossible to forge a perfect copy. Of course, not all would-be crooks sweat the details. In 2004, Alice Pike of Atlanta was arrested after she tried to use a novelty $1 million bill at a Wal-Mart store, apparently not realizing the Treasury doesn't make (and has never made) that denomination.

When All Else Fails

If you've tried all of the above tricks and you're still a little doubtful, there is a last resort: The U.S. Department of the Treasury Test. Although not really applicable to the average cash-using citizen, this test is definitely the most accurate. The U.S. Treasury keeps special currency-analysis machines at its locations around the country, where each machine has 30 different kinds of sensors, most likely trained to spot secret security features only the government knows about.

Coke vs. Pepsi

The Dilemma: You're at a restaurant. You've specifically asked for a Coke when you get handed a Pepsi, or vice versa. You tell the waiter what you requested, and he gives you the "What's the difference?" shrug. Perhaps it's time you laid it on him.

People You Can Impress: "Impressed" probably doesn't accurately reflect the aforementioned waiter's likely response.

The Quick Trick: If you drink them side by side, Pepsi is the sweeter of the two (which is why people tend to prefer Pepsi in the Pepsi Challenge).

The Explanation:

Although the fantastic ad campaigns run by both companies would have you think otherwise, the soft drinks' similarities are pretty striking. For starters, Pepsi and Coke were both the brainchildren of Southern pharmacists. Coca-Cola was invented by Atlantan Dr. John Pemberton in 1886. And yes, there was originally a concentration of cocaine in the soda, but it was reduced to a tiny amount (1/400th of a grain per ounce) by 1902 and removed altogether by 1930. The Coca-Cola Company changed hands a few times, and after Prohibition Coca-Cola was sold to the Woodruff family for $25 million.

Pepsi, on the other hand, was born a few years after Coke. In 1893, pharmacist Caleb Bradham began experimenting with various drink mixtures in New Bern, N.C. His 1898 concoction, then known by the creative name "Brad's Drink," became an overnight success, and "Doc" Bradham began selling his "Exhilarating, Invigorating, Digestion Aiding" syrup by the gallon (7,968 of them for soda fountains in his first year). In the 1940s, Pepsi, as the drink came to be known, adopted a red, white, and blue logo to support America's war effort (or to profit from a hollow, contrived gesture of patriotism—if you're a Coke drinker).

While both drinks contain vanilla, rare oils, carbonated water, kola nut extracts, and the widely beloved high-fructose corn syrup, Coca-Cola maintains a secret ingredient: the mysterious "7X." The formula for the soft drink (including 7X) is kept in a bank vault in Atlanta, and employees who know the secret formula sign nondisclosure agreements before they get to peek at the recipe. In fact, the secret of 7X is so well kept that Coke was for a time forced to abandon the market in India after a law there required that all trade-secret information be disclosed to the government. The law was changed in 1991, and ever since, Coke and Pepsi have been vying for the lion's share of the Indian market.

Soda Myths

1. Neither Coke nor Pepsi will kill you if combined with Pop Rocks.
2. A tooth left in a glass of cola will not dissolve overnight. Nor will a penny, for that matter. And while anything with sugar and acid—orange juice, for instance—will eventually dissolve teeth, it takes quite a while.

Regular Model vs. Supermodel

The Dilemma: Sure, your friend's been on the cover of *Vogue* a couple of times now, but does that make her legitimately super?

People You Can Impress: supermodels!

The Quick Trick: A *model* gets arrested for snorting cocaine; a *supermodel* gets on the cover of *People* for snorting cocaine.

The Explanation:

Like beauty itself, supermodeldom is in the eye of the beholder. One day, perhaps, there will be a Model Sanctioning Body that will establish clear rules for who qualifies as a supermodel—but until then we'll just have to muddle our way through. The difference between regular and super models is generally believed to involve not money but fame: A supermodel is someone whose celebrity extends outside of the fashion world. That is to say, you don't have to know your Dolce from your Gabbana to know that Cindy Crawford is really pretty.

Janice Dickinson, the thrice-divorced *Surreal Life* alum who wrote the literary gem *Everything About Me Is Fake . . . And I'm Perfect,* coined the term *supermodel* in 1979. Hence, she calls herself the world's first supermodel. But we feel that no one who ever appeared on *Surreal Life* should be legally allowed the title of "super" anything. A better candidate for first-ever supermodel might be Suzy Parker. Born in 1932, the 5'10" Parker ushered in the era of tall female models, starred in many ad campaigns, and appeared in the movie *Funny Face* with Fred Astaire. She also became one of the first fashion models to be really, really bad at acting. But being unable to act your way out of a paper bag is just all part of *la vita supermodel*.

Nadja Auermann: Said to have the world's longest legs (they're 45"), Auermann has appeared on many magazine covers, starred in a couple German movies, and has her own perfume. But 1) these days, everybody has her own perfume, and 2) nobody outside of Germany can pronounce her last name. Verdict: **model.**

Naomi Campbell: Instantly recognizable, Campbell's made $50 million modeling, was one of *People*'s 50 Most Beautiful People in 1991, wrote (well, cowrote) a novel, and sold one million copies of her first and only album, *Babywoman*. (It was a failure in America, but a single from it was a huge hit in Japan.) Plus, she used to date Usher. Verdict: **supermodel.**

Helena Christensen: This former Miss Denmark changed our lives forever with her appearance in the music video for Chris Isaak's *Wicked Game*. And she dated Leonardo DiCaprio (although, really, at this point who hasn't?) in addition to appearing on the cover of countless fashion mags. But she never managed to parlay the *Wicked Game* video into widespread renown. Nothing personal, Helena, but we're gonna say: **model.**

Tyson Beckford: A former gangbanger who left the streets behind to become the face of Calvin Klein apparel, Beckford is the highest-paid male model in human history. He also appeared in *Zoolander* and 2003's Oscar-nominated *Biker Boyz*. What's that you say? *Biker Boyz* wasn't nominated for an Oscar? Oh, well. The verdict's still: **supermodel.**

o o o o o o o o o o o

Cordial vs. Liqueur vs. Schnapps

The Dilemma: After several glasses, you don't much care what the difference is, but we're here to tell you anyway!

People You Can Impress: gourmets, gourmands, bartenders, dates, and your more refined alcoholics

The Quick Trick: Liqueurs are for nuts (hazelnuts, almonds), cordials are for fruit (lemon, orange, etc). And schnapps—well, just remember they're not schweetened.

The Explanation:

If you're looking for a basic rule of thumb, try this: Cordials are liquors made from fruit or fruit juice, while liqueurs are alcoholic drinks made from seeds, herbs, or nuts. So triple sec, sloe gin, Grand Marnier, Cointreau, Curaçao, brandy, kir, framboise, and Chambord would all be cordials. On the other hand, Jägermeister, Pernod, Kahlúa, Amaretto, Frangelico, Strega, and Chartreuse are liqueurs. (And for those of you looking for a good time across the pond, beware! In England, the word *cordial* usually refers to a sweetened drink that is *not* alcoholic—Rose's Lime Cordial being a prime example.)

But back to the happy juice. Cordials and liqueurs aside, you've got some drinks that fall into a weird gray area, being made from things that are neither fruits nor nuts nor herbs. Advocaat is a creamy, liqueur made of eggs (i.e., it is both a drink and a hangover cure). And Drambuie is a scotch whisky-based liqueur made with honey, herbs, and spices. Other whiskey-based liqueurs include Bailey's Irish Cream and Southern Comfort (which is cordial-like because it contains fruit, although there's nothing cordial about what it does to your gut).

To further confuse matters, there's a whole category of liqueurs called *anisées*, which are made with anise, which tastes like licorice. Absinthe is the most famous *anisée*. Banned in America because of the hallucinatory wormwood in it, absinthe's traditional nickname is the Green Fairy, which should tell you a bit about its effect on the drinker.

But what about that other syrupy headache inducer, schnapps? Most Americans would think there's no real difference, but Germans would take considerable umbrage at that. True German schnapps are clear, distilled from fruits, and are *not* sweetened. The American versions however, marketed by companies like DeKuyper, are heavily sweetened and unfairly give true schnapps a bad reputation.

Aperitif vs. Digestif

While the line between liqueurs and cordials isn't always clear, the one between apertifs and digestifs is. Simply stated: Aperitifs are for before dinner, to help stimulate the appetite. Classic aperitifs include the Martini, the Manhattan, the Old-Fashioned, and the Sidecar. Digestifs are, obviously, to aid digestion, and are drunk after dinner. If you're aiming to put a bit more class in your act, try closing out your next meal with one of these digestif Hall of Famers: the White (or Black) Russian, the Brandy Alexander, Kahlúa, the Grasshopper, Amaretto, port, or cognac.

Lager vs. Ale

The Dilemma: "Waiter! Bring us another round of that, um, cold and frothy stuff. You know."

People You Can Impress: Germans, Czechs, Packers fans, and possibly beer snobs. Truth be told, though, *nothing* impresses beer snobs—not even other beer snobs. But maybe teenagers will think you're cool.

The Quick Trick: In order to tell the difference, you're going to have to taste the beer. We know: It's a hardship, but it's necessary. An ale typically has a nutty and somewhat bitter taste, while a lager will be mild, fruity, and crisp.

The Explanation:

Beer couldn't be simpler: water, malted barley, yeast, and hops. But from those four ingredients comes a staggering array of varieties.

Lager and ale are the two primary beer categories. Ale originated in Britain. It's brewed at room temperature and tends to contain more hops and malt than lager, which gives it that bitter, nutty taste. Lager, on the other hand, originated in Germany, where it was fermented in cold Bavarian caves. Today it's still brewed at temperatures between 45° and 57°F to give it that crisp flavor. Lagers also have to be stored for a comparatively long amount of time before you can drink them (the word *lager* comes from the German word meaning "to store"). That's good news for mass breweries such as Heineken, Coors, Harp, Beck's, Budweiser, and these writers' personal favorite, Yuengling, brewed in Pottsville, Pa. Plus the yeast used to ferment lager can be reused from one batch to another, so it's more economical than making ale.

As a side note, you should be aware that you can't believe everything you read—even on beer labels. In America, earning the "light" label means a beer must have fewer than 100 calories per serving. But in Canada, "light" refers to a beer that contains between 2.5 and 4 percent alcohol. In other words, a light American beer could be non-light in Canada, and vice versa.

Whazzzzup with Hops?

Hops are the dried flowers of the hop plant, which grows like a vine but is technically called a bine (since it uses hairs to climb, not tendrils). When ripe and harvested they look a bit like soft green pinecones. When and what amount of hops you add to the beer makes a huge difference in taste. Boiling them with the beer makes them very bitter. Adding them after boiling (called dry-hopping), less so. And just as Kentucky is for racehorses, Central Europe is the home of the hop. The four varieties grown there, which are less bitter and more aromatic, are referred to as the "noble hops."

Miracle Whip vs. Mayonnaise

The Dilemma: Two thick white dressings with similar flavor in similar-looking jars are bearing down on you from your refrigerator, and you're asking yourself just one question: "Do I feel lucky?" Well, do ya, punk?

People You Can Impress: deli-goers and anyone killing time in the checkout line

The Quick Trick: Taste them both side by side. The sweeter one is Miracle Whip.

The Explanation:

In 1756, the French under Louis François Armand de Vignerot du Plessis, duc de Richelieu, captured Mahón on the Spanish-held island of Minorca. In honor of this victory, the duc's chef created a new dressing for his master: Mahonnaise. It wasn't until 1905, however, at Richard Hellmann's New York deli, that Americans got to taste the goods. But boy, did it catch on! Within seven years, he'd mass-marketed the condiment as Hellmann's Blue Ribbon Mayonnaise.

To be frank, mayo is one of those love-it-or-hate-it things. The lovers know that, in its most authentic form, mayo's a pretty simple affair: raw egg yolks, oil, lemon juice or vinegar, and spices. Not much room for improvement.

But in 1933, Kraft Foods thought differently. Inventor Charles Chapman's patented emulsifying machine allowed regular mayonnaise to be evenly blended with cheaper dressings and more than 20 different spices (plus sugar). The result was Miracle Whip, which debuted at the 1933 Chicago World's Fair. Promising to create "Salad Miracles with Miracle Whip Salad Dressing," the Whip was an instant hit. (Note: It's not known if the dressing is responsible for any non-salad-related miracles.)

The main differences between Miracle Whip and mayonnaise are the sweeteners: high-fructose corn syrup and sugar are the fourth and fifth ingredients, respectively, of Miracle Whip.

And a Word About Grey Poupon

While we're on the subject of condiments, we couldn't resist the opportunity to squeeze in a quick fact about mustard, or more specifically Grey Poupon. While it sounds hoity-toity, the name Grey Poupon isn't so much about the mustard's color as it is the names of two 18th-century big-time mustard firms from Dijon (run by guys cleverly named Maurice Grey and Antoine Poupon). The name can be a bit confusing, and even unappetizing, to French speakers, as *poupon* means "newborn baby."

o o o o o o o o o o o

Penne vs. Ziti vs. Rigatoni vs. Mostaccioli

The Dilemma: The recipe calls for penne, but all you have is rigatoni. Mama mia!

People You Can Impress: men in the "sanitation business" or women who pinch your cheeks and tell you you're too skinny

The Quick Trick: Who cares? *Mange!*

The Explanation:

Let's start with the word *pasta*. It's so commonplace that you generally don't even think about the word itself. But *pasta* is simply Italian for "paste," the flour-and-water dough from which pasta is made. The fancy culinary term is "alimentary paste." Now you may be thinking, Uncooked pasta's not a *paste*. It's hard until I boil it. That's only because Americans mostly buy dried pasta in boxes. Fresh pasta is actually soft.

Today culinary scientists estimate that there are roughly one bazillion kinds of pasta, or so we've heard. A lot of them are so similar, it makes you wonder why they ever came up with them (can anyone explain why we needed two corkscrew pastas: fusilli *and* rotini? And don't get us started on spiralini). But obviously, a food so central to the Italian lifestyle is going to have lots of variations.

All four of these pastas are tubular, which is why people

get them confused. Like most pastas, they're named after what they look like.

We'll start with the most basic. Ziti are smooth, short tubes. The name comes from the now obsolete word in the Tuscan dialect, *citta,* meaning "girl" or "bride." Some stories claim the pasta got its name because it was often served at weddings. Others say it was named after the masculine version, *citto* ("bridegroom"), because it looks a bit phallic.

Rigatoni, on the other hand, are basically ziti with ridges (from the Italian *rigate*). The theory is that ridged pasta holds on to the sauce better. If your tubes are slightly curved and ridged, however, they're tortiglioni. If the tubes are straight but the ridges are spiral, enjoy your elicoidali, paesan.

Now on to the diagonal tubes. Much like the ridge innovation, the diagonal cuts to the ends of these pastas are meant to be better for scooping up sauce. If a diagonally cut tube is smooth, that's mostaccioli, meaning "little mustache," because at some point little mustaches must have looked more like this. Penne are like mostaccioli, but slightly longer and thinner. As for their meaning, *penne* means "quill pens," the tips of which penne resemble.

Of course, your tubular choices don't exactly end there. You might also enjoy paccheri, maltagliati, canneroni, cannolicchi, reginelle, and pasta al ceppo. And when all else fails, you can't go wrong with elbow macaroni.

Cooking 101

Add a pinch of salt to cooking pasta to keep it firm. Oh, and should you combine different types of pasta in one dish, be sure to use similarly shaped varieties, so that they cook in the same amount of time.

o o o o o o o o o o

Scotch vs. Bourbon

The Dilemma: As you cough a little and rasp, "Smooth!" you're wondering if the burning truck that just hit you was scotch or bourbon.

People You Can Impress: burly men in skirts or old guys in white suits with dogs named Belvedere

The Quick Trick: If it's sweeter, comes from Kentucky, and is spelled "whiskey," it's bourbon. If it's smoky or briny, comes from Scotland, and is spelled "whisky," it's scotch.

The Explanation:

Scotch and bourbon are both whiskeys distilled from grains and aged in oak barrels. But there are very important differences.

Bourbon starts with mash, a ground mix of corn and other grains, usually rye and barley. Bourbon mash must be at least 51 percent corn (if it's a mix of new corn mash and stuff that's been used once before, it's called *sour mash*). This high content of corn and its sugars is why bourbon is so much sweeter than scotch. The mash is *malted* (soaked in water to release the sugars, then heated to stop germination), fermented with yeast, then distilled. The spirit is then aged in oak barrels, the insides of which have been charred. Once the whiskey is removed, that barrel can never be used for bourbon again. The years spent in the barrel give bourbon its caramel color (it actually goes in clear). In order to be called bourbon, a whiskey *must* be made in Kentucky (hence, Jack Daniels Tennessee Whiskey, not Jack Daniels Bourbon).

Scotch whisky, on the other hand (from the Gaelic *uisge beatha,* "the water of life"), is made from malted barley. To stop the germination, the malt is traditionally heated over peat fires, which gives scotch its trademark smokiness. (Peat is basically flammable dirt, cut from huge bogs found all over Scotland.) After distillation, the scotch is aged in barrels called casks, most of which have already been used for bourbons and wines. Connoisseurs look for scotches based on the qualities added by the previous inhabitants of the casks: Sherry casks add a caramel sweetness, Madeira casks add floral notes, etc. The liquor must age at least three years before it can be called scotch. And although similar whiskeys are made in Canada (Crown Royal), Japan (Suntory), and Ireland (Bushmill's, Jameson's), only those from Scotland can bear the prized scotch moniker.

Single Malt vs. Blend

For those of you trying to make an impression, there's an extra complication with scotch: is it *single malt* or *blended?* The distinction is simple. Single malts contain whisky from one distillery at one age. Popular single malts include Macallan, Glenfiddich, Glenlivet, and many others that start with *Glen*. Blended scotch contains whiskeys from various distilleries that've been, well, blended together. Johnnie Walker, Chivas Regal, Cutty Sark, J&B, and Dewar's are all blends. While they're both tasty, connoisseurs lean to single malts because, like wines, they possess more individual character.

Social
Studies

President John Adams vs. President John Q. Adams

The Dilemma: You know they were both presidents, and you probably know that John "No Q" Adams came before John Q. Adams, but you sure couldn't tell them apart in a presidential lineup.

People You Can Impress: the legions of people who read David McCullough's bestselling *John Adams* and the 47 people who read Paul C. Nagel's *John Quincy Adams*

The Quick Trick: John Q, who was the son of Just John, had muttonchops. Also, Q was a completely ineffective president; Adams, a moderately ineffective one.

The Explanation:

While his second cousin Samuel "They Named a Beer for Me" Adams had all the charisma and participated in such rollicking parties as the Boston Tea one, John Adams was a studious lawyer and policy wonk. While Sam dumped tea in the Boston harbor to protest taxes, John was writing letters to the editor opposing the Stamp Act. Yet the wonkish John was popular enough to receive 34 electoral college votes in the U.S.'s first presidential election in 1789. George Washington got 69 (no snickering), and was elected president—Adams, having finished second, was given the post of vice president.

Unfortunately, Mr. Adams didn't think much of the gig, saying, "My country has in its wisdom contrived for me the most insignificant office that ever the invention of man contrived. . . ." Despite his overuse of the word *contrived,* Adams managed to win the presidential election of 1797. Adams's primary accomplishment was almost getting America into a war with France after a French minister was rude to an American envoy. Soon after, he was defeated in the election of 1800 by his vice president, Thomas Jefferson—making John Adams the first-ever one-term president.

Adams's son John Q. followed in his proud father's footsteps by becoming the second-ever one-term president. After a stellar career as a diplomat, John Q. ran for president in 1824. And although he lost both the popular and electoral vote, no one won a majority, so the election went to the House of Representatives, where John Q. made enough friends to be declared prez. John Q. had a lot of interesting ideas—he wanted to start a federal highway system and a national public university, for instance. Unfortunately, he had his father's lack of charisma, and could never convince Congress or the American public of the value of his policies. Q. was soundly defeated in 1828 by Andrew Jackson, but he ended up not getting fired from government so much as suffering a demotion. He served in the House of Representatives from 1831 to his death in 1848, where he proved to be a far better congressman than president. In fact, he spent much of his congressional career trying to end slavery.

o o o o o o o o o o

Aztec vs. Inca

The Dilemma: You're pretty sure both these ancient civilizations were located north of Antarctica and south of Dallas—but that's about all you know.

People You Can Impress: It's not so much a matter of impressing people as it is not embarrassing yourself when chatting up armchair historians.

The Quick Trick: The dominant ethnic group in the Aztec empire were the Mexica (pron. meh-SHEE-kuh), hence Mexico. The Inca empire was centered in what is today Peru.

The Explanation:

It's easy to confuse your Aztecs with your Incans because they have a great deal in common: Both empires reached their peaks in the early 16th century, both made huge technological and scientific discoveries, both dabbled in the delicate art of human sacrifice, and both suffered mightily at the hands of Spanish conquistadors.

As for differences, though, the easiest distinction is geography. The Inca empire controlled parts of modern-day Chile, Peru, Argentina, Ecuador, Bolivia, and Colombia. The Aztecs, meanwhile, set up camp more than 1,000 miles to the north. To protect themselves from invaders, the Aztecs built their capital city, Tenochtitlán, on a large island in the middle of Lake Texcoco. These days, Mexico City stands upon the ruins of Tenochtitlán. (As for the lake, almost all of the water has been drained to make room for suburbs.)

Between 1375 and 1521, the Aztecs built a thriving empire with influence that extended throughout the area that is today's Mexico. The Aztecs were among the world's first people to require education for all children (even girls!) regardless of social standing. Of course, girls were not taught how to read and write at school (the Aztecs were ahead of their time, sure—but girls reading and writing? That's crazy talk); their education was focused on home and children. In 1521, the Aztecs were conquered by Spanish conquistador Hernán Cortés, who defeated them partly by giving them smallpox and partly by raising an army of 200,000 indigenous people opposed to Aztec rule.

As for the Incas, their empire started out as a small tribe, but beginning in 1438, they rapidly expanded through the Andes mountain range, eventually controlling most of the western coast of South America. Their empire was notable for its diversity: More than 700 languages were spoken in Incan land, and the empire never really coalesced into a single political entity. In the end, the Incas never got the chance to build a lasting civilization, mainly because in 1532, Francisco Pizarro showed up. With only 200 men and 27 horses, Pizarro should have been crushed. But, like Cortés, he had two things working to his favor: smallpox and thousands of indigenous people resentful of Incan rule.

Both empires' stories finish sadly—but then neither Pizarro nor Cortés fared all that well, either. Pizarro was assassinated in 1541, and Cortés spent much of his later life suffering from bouts of insane paranoia.

o o o o o o o o o o o

Serial Killer vs. Mass Murderer

The Dilemma: The guy sitting next to you at the bar keeps insisting that John Wayne Gacy wasn't a serial killer but a mass murderer, which is really creepy. But is he right?

People You Can Impress: authors of true crime novels and suckers for semantics

The Quick Trick: The creepy guy at the bar is full of it: Gacy was a serial killer because he committed many murders over a long period of time; mass murderers commit many murders all at once.

The Explanation:

The difference here is all about the details—but then, any *CSI* fan knows that the magic of police work is in the little things. According to the U.S. Department of Justice, Statistics Bureau (and yes, there really is such a thing), "mass murder" is a single event at one location involving the murder of four or more people. Kill three people at once, therefore, and you're merely a homicidal jerk. Terrorism and government-sanctioned murder often are considered mass murder.

Serial killers, on the other hand, kill in a *series* of events. The killers usually don't know their victims (the opposite is true with mass murderers), they almost always have "cooling off" periods between murders, and they usually derive sexual excitement from the killings. To qualify as a serial killer, one needs three victims. It rather goes without saying, but serial killers tend to be pretty screwed up individuals. Although there are records of serial killers going back to at least 1400, the term wasn't coined until the 1970s, when killers Ted Bundy and David "Son of Sam" Berkowitz were frequently in the news.

SERIAL KILLERS

Gilles de Rais (1404–1440): Once one of the richest men in France, Rais raped, tortured, and murdered between 80 and 200 boys—and a few girls—on the grounds of his various estates.

Long before there was Aileen "*Monster*" Wuornos, there was **Elizabeth "the Bloody Lady" Bathory** (1560–1614). Some sources claim that Bathory, a Hungarian countess, tortured and killed *2,000* young girls (mostly peasants, but some lower gentry).

When it comes to British serial killers in the 19th century, Jack the Ripper gets all the press. But **Mary Ann Cotton** (1832–1873) was more prolific, killing as many as 21 people. Cotton probably poisoned four of her husbands, a variety of her friends and in-laws, and several of her own children with arsenic.

MASS MURDERERS

The term "going postal" has its roots in the case of one **Patrick Sherrill**, a disgruntled former postman who walked into the post office in Edmond, Ill. on August 20, 1986, and killed 14 employees before committing suicide.

On November 1, 1955, **Jack Gilbert Graham** put his mother on a flight from Denver to Portland with a dynamite bomb in her suitcase. (Graham wanted her life insurance money.) The bomb exploded midair, killing all 44 people aboard.

o o o o o o o o o o o

NASDAQ Composite Index vs. Dow Jones Industrial Average

The Dilemma: You want to get rich quick, but you don't really want to work. So what's the appropriate index for you?

People You Can Impress: people in suits

The Quick Trick: Unless you're reading this book in 2037 and times have drastically changed, the NASDAQ Composite Index is lower than the Dow Jones Industrial Average.

The Explanation:

The DJIA was created by former *Wall Street Journal* cofounder Charles Dow in 1896. Dow picked 12 important companies from a variety of industries, from the U.S. Leather Company to the American Sugar Company (things had more transparent names in the days before Exelon). The only company still on the list is General Electric. Today the average includes not 12 companies but 30, from 3M to Wal-Mart. When first published, the DJIA stood at 40.94. The DJIA hadn't closed above 1,000 until 1972. But the '80s and '90s were periods of intense growth for the stock market as a whole, which was reflected in the Average: By January of 2000, just before the dot-com bust, the average reached 11,722.98.

Although it only reflects what's happening to a tiny percentage of publicly traded companies, the DJIA has been an important measure of the stock market's health for more than a century, and it's unlikely to go anywhere. There are broader, more accurate reflections of what's happening (like the S&P 500 index), but at the end of the day, the most attention is still paid to the DJIA.

That's starting to change, however, thanks largely to the NASDAQ. Most DJIA companies are traded on the New York Stock Exchange; the NASDAQ exchange is a relative newcomer to the stock exchange game (it was founded in 1971), and was the world's first fully electronic stock market. As befits a digital stock exchange, many of NASDAQ's marquis stocks are tech companies, including Microsoft, Amazon.com, and Dell. The NASDAQ Composite Index is an alternative to the DJIA. Instead of measuring the peaks and troughs of 30 big companies, it measures the change in the more than 3,000 stocks traded on NASDAQ. Because it's a tech-heavy stock exchange, it suffered much worse than the DJIA after the dot-com bust, falling from 5,132 to a low below 1,200 in 2002. Still, the NASDAQ Composite Index started back in 1971 with a value of exactly 100—so it's done well overall. If there are any lessons to be drawn from the histories of both DJIA and NASDAQ, it is these: Long-term investors tend to make more money. And, perhaps most important, investors who start out rich tend to get richer.

o o o o o o o o o o

Murder vs. Manslaughter

The Dilemma: You have this, uh, friend. Yeah, that's it—a friend. And he's gotten himself into a little bit of a, um, predicament. He just needs some legal advice, that's all.

People You Can Impress: the whole gang down in Cell Block C. Love you guys!

The Quick Trick: Did your "friend" plan the crime ahead of time? If so, it's murder.

The Explanation:

Most of the world's legal systems distinguish between cold-blooded killings, crimes of passion, and accidental (but still unlawful) deaths. In America, "murder" applies to deaths involving some period of premeditation. But this is a little problematic, because the period of forethought and planning can comprise years or a fraction of a second. Technically, all purposeful crimes involve some measure of premeditation—i.e., there's always a moment between your brain sending the signal to shoot and your hand squeezing the trigger. So it falls to the jury to decide what constitutes adequate forethought and planning to be called murder. The typical sentence for murder in America is either 25 years in prison or life without the possibility of parole; only about 2.5 percent of murders nationwide result in death sentences.

If it's not quite murder, but was still done on purpose, then it might be "voluntary manslaughter." (Take the classic example of the cuckolded husband who catches his wife in the sack with another man and snaps.) Known as "Man 1" on the 37 varieties of *Law & Order,* voluntary manslaughter generally results in a sentence between 15 and 20 years in prison. A third category, "involuntary manslaughter," covers situations in which the killing is neither planned nor intentional—for instance, convincing your buddy that riding his bike off a cliff would be totally rad. The most common variety of involuntary manslaughter stems from drunk driving: In 2004, 16,694 Americans were killed in alcohol-related car crashes.

It May Be a Small World . . .

. . . but criminal law still differs widely from nation to nation:

In Japan, the worst sentences are reserved for people who kill their own descendants.

In Italy, punishments may be lessened if killers can prove they acted to avenge their honor.

Murder Was the Case That They Gave Me

"187" has become ubiquitous slang for murder thanks to rappers like Snoop Dogg (who was once acquitted of murder). Why? Section 187 of the California Penal Code covers murder—but that's not always the case. In Texas, for instance, murder isn't a 187 but a 19.03, which doesn't roll off the tongue quite as well.

o o o o o o o o o o

World Bank vs. the International Monetary Fund

The Dilemma: Thanks to your poor credit, *another* bank just turned down your loan application. You're thinking of declaring yourself an independent nation and seeking financial help from one of these two organizations. But which one is most likely to cough up some cash?

People You Can Impress: dictators of the developing world, international financiers, and hotties wearing turtle outfits at G8 summit protests

The Quick Trick: The Bank lends you money; the Fund concerns itself with nations' exchange rates and fiscal policies.

The Explanation:

Don't feel bad if you can't tell these institutions apart. They were created at the same time, in July of 1944, in the tiny New Hampshire village of Bretton Woods. And no less an economist than John Maynard Keynes, whom both the World Bank and the IMF see as a founding father, found the names confusing: He felt the Bank should be called a Fund and the Fund a Bank.

The International Monetary Fund was created primarily to avert future Great Depressions, in the hopes that preventing depressions would prevent world wars starring an angry Germany. The IMF seeks to promote stability both internationally and within member nations by requiring open access to currency exchange, encouraging free trade (which has earned the ire of protestors both in America and the developing world), and preventing the wild fluctuations in currency value that preceded World War II. The IMF also maintains an actual fund of money, which it uses to help bail out nations that abide by its policies but still find themselves in dire economic straits.

The World Bank, on the other hand, is properly known as the International Bank for Reconstruction and Development, which is a fairly good description of what it does. Initially created to help rebuild the economies of postwar Europe (which was a bit ambitious, since it was created several months *before* the war in Europe ended), the World Bank now seeks to build infrastructure by giving low-interest loans to nations in the developing world.

Both institutions are controversial for more or less the same reason: Their ostensible goal is to help economically troubled nations develop and stabilize, but critics say that they really do the opposite. The World Bank saddles them with more debt, and the IMF hurts the poor with its emphasis on free international trade. But advocates of the system, and there are many, argue that free trade and cheap infrastructure will make both economic and political stability more feasible throughout the world. We've avoided another world war thus far, anyway.

o o o o o o o o o o

Hasidic Jew vs. Orthodox Jew

The Dilemma: Here you are, 30 years old, and you feel like such a *schmendrick* because you don't know your *bubkes* from your *tochis*.

People You Can Impress: everyone at the bar mitzvah

The Quick Trick: Ask the person next to you what he or she thinks about reincarnation. Hasidic Judaism is a more mystical and emotional spirituality that includes beliefs in prophetic dreams, miracles, spiritual healing, and—yes—the Big R. Of course, there's also the attire. Most Hasidic Jews wear black robes called *bekishe,* nicely accessorized with a *gartel,* or prayer belt.

The Explanation:

Hasidic and Orthodox Jews both believe Old Testament laws and other sacred Jewish writings are 100 percent applicable today. In fact, Hasidic Jews used to be Orthodox Jews—right up until the 18th century. By contrast, other Jewish sects believe the rules were only meant for the time period in which they were written.

That's when a Polish worker named Israel ben Eliezer began preaching that anyone could communicate with God, not just the learned men who studied religious texts. To Ben Eliezer, emotional and mystical piety were just as important as the scholarly spirituality of Orthodox Judaism, if not more so. His sect eventually came to be called Hasidism (or Chasidism), from the Hebrew word meaning "pious." By the mid-19th century, most Jews in the Ukraine were Hasidic, and a number of sects within sects developed out of Ben Eliezer's teachings. However, all the varieties of Hasidism emphasize close communion with an omnipresent God and a kabbalah-influenced mysticism.

With their distinct dress, Hasidic Jews are pretty hard to miss, and that's part of the point. They believe their faith separates them from the general population and that their style of dress should reflect this distinction. It's also an expression of their commitment to tradition, as their dress today was typical for Ukrainian Jews 250 years ago. Male Hasidic Jews also sometimes sport long beards and curled sideburns called *payot*, based on a biblical commandment barring men from shaving the sides of their faces.

Orthodox Jews and Vulcans—What's the Similarity?

The split-fingered Vulcan salute from *Star Trek* is actually derived from an Orthodox ritual, the Blessing Hands used to anoint congregations on holy days. *Star Trek* icon Leonard Nimoy, who was raised in the Orthodox tradition, adapted the hand gesture for his role as Mr. Spock.

o o o o o o o o o o

Communism vs. Socialism

The Dilemma: Ever since they took the rod out of the Iron Curtain and sent communism to the cleaners, your knowledge of competing political philosophies has blurred.

People You Can Impress: your ninth-grade civics teacher and Fidel Castro

The Quick Trick: Just toss socialism around in conversation and you're guaranteed to be right.

The Explanation:

While both terms basically mean that property and the means of production are being shared for the good of the people, socialism is much more loosely defined and, as such, encompasses communism. The spectrum of socialism is pretty wide, from social democracies like Sweden to societies where the state assumes responsibility for all economic planning, like the Soviet Union back when it was the Soviet Union. The idea, put simply, is cooperation instead of competition.

More specifically, communism has evolved from the Greeks (Plato advocated a world of communal bliss and harmony without private property) to Sir Thomas More's *Utopia* to Karl Marx and Friedrich Engels's *Communist Manifesto* to Vladimir Lenin's Russian revolution. Much of the theory for communism grew out of discontent in the wake of the Industrial Revolution. Blue-collar workers were often treated appallingly, and the idea of a classless society with shared resources seemed ideal. In fact, Engels and Marx predicted that when economic forces became insufferable, the lower classes would revolt to create a communist state. Well, maybe not. While there are quite a few social democracies extant today, communist strongholds are few and far between.

Good to Know

Oddly enough, Adam Smith's bible of capitalism, *Wealth of Nations*—often quoted with authority by proponents of small government—actually advocates a somewhat socialist brand of democracy. Smith, who famously coined the term "invisible hand" to describe the way in which looking out for number one magically equates to looking out for the whole community, also recognized that increased wealth alone would not make for healthy communities.

Seeing Red: American Communists

In the 1950s, *everyone* was accused of belonging to the Communist Party. But these folks actually did:

John Dos Passos
Langston Hughes
Pete Seeger
Richard Wright
Elia Kazan
W.E.B. DuBois

o o o o o o o o o o

Cathedral vs. Basilica vs. Shrine

The Dilemma: You're looking to go to a Catholic church, but as it happens, you don't know your mass from your elbow.

People You Can Impress: popes, cardinals, priests, bishops, ministers, deacons, nuns, altar boys, and your really, really devout grandmother

The Quick Trick: The quickest trick is just to call everything "church."

The Explanation:

In the days of old Rome, *basilica* referred to any public building built in the shape of a rectangle with a main aisle down the middle and flanking aisles separated by columns (i.e., from above, it looks like a cross). Once Rome became Christianized, a lot of these buildings were converted into churches. So if a church was built in this style, it can rightly be called a basilica. Unless, of course, it's a Roman Catholic church.

Why? Roman Catholic basilicas must be designated as such by the pope himself! Just to clarify, a regular church can get called up to the majors if it has particular spiritual or historical significance to the capital-C Church. The granddaddy of all basilicas, for instance, is St. Peter's, one of seven major basilicas in Rome.

Unlike regular churches, basilicas have special trappings as traditional emblems of their basilica-ness. One is the *conopaeum*, an umbrella-like fixture with silk panels of red and yellow, symbolically used to shelter His Holiness in the event of a visit. More important, each Catholic basilica has a door designated as its "holy door." This door, being holy and all, is opened only on special occasions. Hence, it was a pretty big deal when Pope John Paul II ordered all the holy doors open for the entire year 2000. (We can only imagine the ungodly heating bills.)

To add a pinch more confusion: Some basilicas are also cathedrals. A cathedral is the home church of a bishop or archbishop.

So what's a shrine, then? Simple: A shrine is a holy spot (usually a church) where something very holy has happened (a person was martyred or a holy apparition seen) or a holy relic is housed (say, a saint's pinky toe—see below). Canterbury Cathedral in England, for instance, is a shrine because St. Thomas Becket was martyred there.

If you haven't figured it out already, some churches are lucky enough to be all three. But you don't have to go to Rome to stumble upon the trifecta. Just hit up the Basilica of the National Shrine of the Assumption of the Blessed Virgin Mary in Baltimore the next time you're looking to confess in style.

The Saintliest Thing in Pittsburgh

The largest collection of relics outside of the Vatican is actually located in Pittsburgh, Pa. In the 19th century, a priest and doctor named Suitbert (Suitbert!) Mollinger became the parish priest at St. Anthony's in Pittsburgh, and he soon took to gathering relics. In fact, by his death in 1892, he had 5,000 of them—from St. Anthony's tooth to St. Ursula's femur. And that's all in the days before eBay!

o o o o o o o o o o o

State vs. Commonwealth

The Dilemma: You know your sharks from your jets and your Rodgers from your Hammersteins. But what in God's name is a commonwealth?

Materials Needed: a map of the U.S. and its territories. Just don't call 'em colonies!

People You Can Impress: geography buffs or any proud residents of four of our medium-sized, heavily accented states

The Quick Trick: There're only four commonwealths, so just memorize 'em, willya? If you can remember John, Paul, George, and Ringo, you can swing MA, PA, VA, and KY.

The Explanation:

There are fifty states in the U.S., but four of them—Pennsylvania, Kentucky, Virginia, and Massachusetts—officially call themselves commonwealths. And the difference between a commonwealth and a state is, well, nothing. Constitutionally speaking, they're identical.

Understanding why these states chose the commonwealth moniker and continue to stick to it so proudly is a lot easier once you consider the history of those states. The original meaning of the word *commonwealth* was a nation or body governed by the people, not some king or tyrant. In fact, the time in British history during which Cromwell and Parliament ruled instead of a king is known as the Commonwealth Period. So when it came time for the American colonies to throw off the yokes of oppression and tea taxes and the excessive use of the letter *u* in words like *colour,* the three hotbeds of revolution—Massachusetts, Pennsylvania, and Virginia—were most eager to signal the difference in government. Perhaps remembering the Commonwealth Period, they declared themselves commonwealths. So what about Kentucky? Kentucky had once been merely a giant western county of Virginia (before that, it was called Transylvania). When it started doing its own thing in 1790, Kentucky kept the commonwealth status. Not to mention the whiskey.

But surprisingly enough, those four states aren't the only ones in our happy American family that are commonwealths. Puerto Rico and the Northern Mariana Islands also go by the moniker. In this context, it means that they have certain rights under the U.S. Constitution and fall under our protection, but they don't qualify for the full benefits of statehood—meaning they don't get any senators and they also don't get to eat deep-fried Twinkies, because they don't get to have state fairs. (Kentucky, on the other hand, has a state fair each August, apparently unperturbed by the fact that it is not, technically, a state.)

State of Dissatisfaction

After the commonwealth of Virginia seceded from the Union in 1861, several northwestern Virginia counties went ahead and seceded from the seceders, choosing instead to stay in the Union. Those counties formed the *state* of West Virginia, feeling no compunction to keep the commonwealth label.

o o o o o o o o o o o

Crazy Horse vs. Sitting Bull vs. Geronimo

The Dilemma: You've heard the names, but can't pick them out of a lineup. And your ignorance only worsens the guilt you already feel about smallpox and land theft.

People You Can Impress: Native Americans tired of having their history confused, conflated, and occasionally made into Kevin Costner movies

The Quick Trick: Group the animal names together: Sitting *Bull* and Crazy *Horse* were Sioux who fought at Little *Bighorn*. Geronimo was an Apache.

The Explanation:

Two of these famous Native American warriors are known to us for helping Custer have his Last Stand at Little Bighorn (June 15, 1876). Sitting Bull and Crazy Horse were both members of Lakota Sioux tribes. And the latter (and supposedly zanier) of the two was known for going into battle without war paint or headdress, instead just rubbing himself with dirt. Despite their contribution to the Custer massacre, both warriors were granted amnesty by the U.S. government. In fact, Crazy Horse was even made an officer in the U.S. Indian Scouts and invited to meet President Rutherford B. Hayes (although he declined). Today a memorial to Crazy Horse is being built in the Black Hills of South Dakota—though it's been under construction since 1948! The original sculptor, Korczak Ziolkowski, died in 1982. When it's finally finished though, the equestrian sculpture will be over 600 feet long and nearly as tall, making it the largest statue in the world.

As for Sitting Bull, the warrior spent four months in 1885 touring with Buffalo Bill Cody's Wild West Show, delighting audiences by swearing at them in his native tongue. While this hardly seems a life for such a noteworthy American, his end was even more tragic. Sitting Bull was killed in 1890 while being arrested for fear he would take part in the Ghost Dance, a ceremony performed to rid the land of white people and restore their way of life to Indians.

As for Geronimo, he was from a different region (the Southwest) and tribe (Apache). In fact, Geronimo was actually a shaman—or medicine man—who fought for years against white settlers, side by side with that other famous Apache warrior, Cochise. When he finally surrendered in 1886, it had taken 5,000 troops a year to corral him and his small band of followers. But the white establishment embraced Geronimo once he was captured: He became a bona fide A-list celebrity, even riding in Teddy Roosevelt's 1905 inaugural parade. He died of pneumonia in 1909 and is buried at Fort Sill, Okla.

Geronimo!

Ever wonder why skydivers shout "Geronimo!" when they jump? Especially since the Apache leader never skydived? The tradition comes from U.S. paratroopers training at Fort Benning in 1940. The night before their first jump, they watched the 1939 film *Geronimo*. To psych themselves up for the jump out of a perfectly good airplane, they shouted his name.

o o o o o o o o o o

Ireland vs. Northern Ireland

The Dilemma: You're in a pub somewhere in the Emerald Isle. A friendly local buys you a pint. Should you toast the queen or the pope?

People You Can Impress: Catholics and Protestants (probably not at the same time)

The Quick Trick: Northern Ireland is part of the UK and largely Protestant. The rest is the Republic of Ireland and mostly Catholic.

The Explanation:

Ireland isn't all jigs and shamrocks and brilliant literature. The island has a long, sad history of religious and political conflict, of British dominion and the Irish quest for home rule. In fact, since the 1960s, the situation has been simply dubbed "the Troubles."

Basically, Ireland's nine northernmost counties constitute the province of Ulster. Six of these—Tyrone, Antrim, Armagh, Londonderry, Down, and Fermanagh—make up Northern Ireland (capital: Belfast), which is subject to the British Crown. But there's a problem. About a quarter of the people in Northern Ireland, mostly Catholics, see the British as an occupying power. They're called Nationalists or Republicans, and they want a united, independent Ireland free of British rule. The rest, mostly Protestants, prefer the status quo. They are called Unionists or Loyalists.

The rest of the island is an independent country, known as

the Republic of Ireland, with its capital at Dublin. This situation has existed since 1922, when the Irish Free State was formed. The Republic's tricolor flag represents its turbulent history: green for the native Catholic population; orange for the Protestants, supporters of William of Orange; and white for peace between the two. Sadly, the colors have coexisted better on the flag than on the island.

The Troubles are reenacted in a small way in Glasgow, Scotland, whenever the city's two main soccer teams meet. Most of the Protestants in Northern Ireland were originally from Scotland (they're called Scots-Irish or Ulster Scots), and the rivalry between the Glasgow Rangers (the Protestant team) and Celtic (the Catholic team) is said to be the bitterest on Earth. (Imagine if the Yankees and the Red Sox blamed each other for centuries of violence and hostility.) The matches and their aftermaths have been marred by riots and even deaths. Historically, Rangers players were forbidden from making the sign of the cross or dating Catholic girls. But in a sign of progress, the Rangers can now make out with whomever they want—and Northern Ireland has thankfully seen a spot of peace since 2000.

The IRA vs. Sinn Féin

Sinn Féin (pronounced "shin FAYN," Gaelic for "we ourselves") is the collective name for various political parties and movements that want independence from England. The Provisional Sinn Féin, or Irish Republican Army, or IRA, or Provos, is a paramilitary (opponents would say terrorist) organization known for its violent resistance to the British presence. In 2005, the IRA renounced violence and began to disarm. Pessimistic historians, however, point to the fact that the Troubles often have a way of being resurrected.

o o o o o o o o o o o

Taoism vs. Confucianism

The Dilemma: A wise man once said . . . wait, which wise man was it?

People You Can Impress: philosophy professors and Miss Manners

The Quick Trick: Confucianism is a system of ethics, and Tao is a path of behavior. Also, Confucius was probably an actual person; Lao-tzu probably wasn't.

The Explanation:

Taoism and Confucianism are two of China's oldest and most pervasive philosophies. They arose during roughly the same period in Chinese history, called the Hundred Schools of Thought, a time often marred by unrest and feudal strife. Both philosophies reflect this, as their overarching goals are to seek order and harmony in one's life, relationship with society, and the universe (oh, is that all?).

Taoism is based on one of several philosophical constructs of right and wrong, light and dark, knowledge and truth called the tao (pronounced DOW, meaning "The Way"). Capital-T Taoism is based on the *Tao Te Ching* ("The Doctrine of the Way and its Virtue," or something that translates roughly like that) attributed to Lao-tzu, who, if he existed, lived sometime between the seventh and fourth centuries BCE. Akin to Buddhism, Taoism seeks to describe the harmonious way to relate to oneself, others, nature, and the universe. One of the head-twisty things about the *Tao Te Ching* is that it never specifically defines The Way. It's a series of verses, poems, and riddles. It emphasizes control but not dominance, fluidity but not ambivalence, and mystery but not confusion. It's full of helpful nuggets, like "Those with simple needs will find them fulfilled," and "To glorify wealth, power, and beauty is to inspire theft, jealousy, and shame." In its course, it's also inspired some modern, pop culture–based philosophical treatises like *The Tao of Homer* (as in Simpson) and *The Te* [Virtue] *of Piglet*.

Confucianism is a philosophy from the same period and can be considered the other side of the Taoist coin. Confucius is the Latinized name of its founder, whose real name was the much more martial arts–sounding K'ung-Fu-tzu. His teachings and lectures are compiled in *The Analects*. Similar to Proverbs in the Old Testament or parables in the New, the analects depend heavily on analogy and metaphor. They stress the importance not of rules per se, but of *ethics*, that guide behavior. Our Golden Rule, the whole "do unto others" thing, comes first from Confucius (even though he wouldn't have called it a "rule"). He also stressed the need for ritual and music. During the Han dynasty (206 BCE –220 CE), his teachings became the official political system of China. But its emphasis on ethics instead of laws often led to corruption. And though the Communists squashed it, it's making a comeback as a code of conduct in modern China.

o o o o o o o o o o

Hitler vs. Himmler vs. Goebbels vs. Göring

The Dilemma: You've seen so many documentaries about these guys, but you still can't tell them apart. They're just so identically *evil.*

People You Can Impress: World War II buffs and fourth-grade history teachers

The Quick Trick: Everybody recognizes Hitler. The one with the Hitler mustache that isn't Hitler is Himmler (he also had glasses). The one with slicked-back hair and mustard-colored jacket is Goebbels. And the fatty in the dove-gray uniform? That's Göring.

The Explanation:

We don't need to tell you anything more about Hitler, *der Führer* (leader) of the Third Reich. After all, he's one of history's scariest figures, and the facts about him have probably been drummed into you since grade school. What you might not know, however, is that a lot of the evil he oversaw was actually committed by his closest henchmen, equally sinister in their own right.

Heinrich Himmler (1900–1945) was one of Hitler's earliest supporters, so in 1929 Hitler chose him to head the SS, the military arm of the Nazi party. What began as a small offshoot of the SA (the party's stormtroopers) became under

Himmler a massive organization of the party's ideological elite, with its own military units (the Waffen-SS) fighting alongside the regular German army (the Wehrmacht). The SS were the perpetrators of the worst Nazi crimes, including the death camps, the mass execution of civilians, and the Gestapo secret police. Amazingly, when the war started to go south, Himmler actually tried to secretly negotiate peace with the British and Americans. Captured by the Brits, he poisoned himself before he could stand trial at Nuremberg.

Joseph Goebbels (pronounced GHERR-buls, 1897–1945) was the Third Reich's propaganda minister. A fiery orator like his boss, Goebbels championed the technique of repeating a Big Lie again and again until people believed it. Known to his enemies as "The Malicious Dwarf," Goebbels spent his last days in Hitler's bunker under Berlin. After Hitler's death, however, Goebbels moved up in rank. He was chancellor of Germany for one whole day. Of course, his happiness was short-lived. While still in Hitler's bunker, his wife, Magda, a Nazi zealot, poisoned six of their children rather than have them live in a world without National Socialism (their oldest child, curiously, survived because he was off fighting). Goebbels proceeded to shoot Magda before turning the gun on himself.

Hermann Göring (1893–1946) led the German Air Force, the Luftwaffe. A decorated World War I hero, he oversaw the air arm of the conquest of Europe until famously squandering his fleet in the Battle of Britain. A drug addict and alcoholic who worried obsessively about his looks, Göring's vanity couldn't keep him from overeating: He seemed to gain 10 pounds every time the Nazis lost a battle. Like Himmler, he was expelled from the Nazi Party by Hitler for suspected treason. And he was sentenced to death by hanging at Nuremberg, but managed to poison himself shortly before the execution.

o o o o o o o o o o o

Roman Empire vs. Holy Roman Empire

The Dilemma: You really like that show on HBO—but which empire is it about?

People You Can Impress: German guys with Roman numerals after their names

The Quick Trick: The Roman Empire was Roman, then moved to Constantinople. The Holy Roman Empire was mostly Germanic, and ruled Central Europe between Charlemagne and Napoléon.

The Explanation:

The Roman Empire (31 BCE–476 CE in the West, and to 1453 in the East) is pretty self-explanatory: It was the empire whose capital was Rome. At its height it stretched from Scotland to the Persian Gulf and all the way around the Mediterranean. But it was always centered on Rome, right? Not so fast.

In 330 CE, the Emperor Constantine, the first emperor to convert to Christianity, moved the capital east to Byzantium and changed its name to Constantinople (a.k.a. Istanbul). Why Constantinople? Because if you're going to found a capital city, you might as well show some good old-fashioned Christian humility and name it after yourself. In the fourth century, the empire officially split in two, with Rome being one capital and Constantinople the other. Then, when Rome was sacked in 476 CE, the western half ceased to be. So Rome was no longer part of the Roman Empire. As for the Holy Roman Empire, you may remember the Mike Myers "Coffee Talk" bit (cribbed from Voltaire) on *Saturday Night Live:* "The Holy Roman Empire was neither holy nor Roman nor an empire. Discuss." Well, that's mostly true.

On Christmas Day, 800 CE, the pope revived the Roman title of emperor and bestowed it on Charlemagne. That's where the "Roman" comes from. But the empire (like Charlemagne) was really Germanic. In fact, it was considered the first German Reich (the second stretched from the unification under Bismarck through World War I. And let's not get into the third one). Charlemagne's successors would eventually rule most of Central Europe, including modern-day Germany, Poland, Austria, the Czech Republic, the Low Countries, parts of France and Italy, and more.

Until its official dissolution in 1806, the Holy Roman Empire was never a single unified state, but more a hodgepodge of hundreds of kingdoms and principalities unified under the Holy Roman emperor, who sometimes inheredited the job and sometimes was elected to it.

Two dynasties stand out as rulers of the empire. The Hohenstaufens led the empire during the Crusades. In fact, it was because of the Crusades that Frederick II dubbed his empire "Holy." In the 13th century, however, the Hohenstaufens were replaced by the Hapsburgs, who were all over the thrones of Europe for the next 800 years or so. In the process, they won the award for Most Thoroughly Inbred Royal Family Ever.

o o o o o o o o o o

Shia vs. Sunni

The Dilemma: Despite hearing news about the Middle East every day, you still don't know Shia from shinola.

People You Can Impress: Iranians, Iraqis, Syrians, Jordanians, and TV talking heads

The Quick Trick: The Shia believe that the early succession of power should have gone like the name of a very famous boxer: 1) Muhammad, 2) Ali.

The Explanation:

Like Christianity, Islam is home to a spectrum of sects espousing different beliefs and practices. And just as Christianity can be divided into two large groups—Catholic and Protestant—from which other subsects have emerged, so too with Islam: Shia and Sunni.

Unlike Christianity, whose major split wouldn't occur for nearly sixteen centuries, Islam split almost immediately after the death of its founder, the Prophet Muhammad (circa 570–632 CE). The rift stems from a disagreement among Muslims over who was the rightful successor to Muhammad.

After the prophet's death on June 8, 632, a gathering of his followers met at Medina and proclaimed Abu Bakr (kinsman, companion, and early convert of Muhammad) caliph, or political leader. The claim stemmed from his close relationship with Muhammad, and the fact that Muhammad had asked Abu Bakr to lead prayers when too ill to do so himself. Those who recognize Abu Bakr and his three immediate successors, called the Four Rightly Guided Caliphs, are referred to as Sunni Muslims, and today almost 90 percent of Muslims worldwide fall into this category.

One group of followers, however, refused to accept Abu Bakr. These Rafidi ("Refusers") supported the claim of Ali ibn Abi Talib, Muhammad's cousin (and son-in-law). The claim is based on a sermon the Prophet had given at Ghadir Khum, in which Muhammad referred to Ali as *mawla,* which some translate as "master." Ali's supporters called themselves Shiat Ali (the Party of Ali), though today they are known as simply Shia. Ali did eventually ascend as the fourth caliph. To Sunni, he is the last of the Four Rightly Guided Caliphs. But to Shias, he is the first caliph and, more important, the first Imam—a word Shia Muslims use to refer to the person chosen leader of all the faithful. While they and the Sunnis both revere the Koran, they accept different hadiths (oral traditions), so their laws are different. Many Shias, for example, allow temporary marriage. Shias also recognize esteemed imams as supreme experts on Islamic law, called Ayatollahs or, for the *really* big guys, Grand Ayatollahs. As for the locations where Shias have a significant Muslim majority, there are really only two: Iraq and Iran.

Much is made of the differences between Shias and Sunnis, but almost all the violence between them in the past 50 years has been caused, directly or indirectly, by Saddam Hussein—a nominal Sunni who by his own admission was never religious.

○ ○ ○ ○ ○ ○ ○ ○ ○ ○ ○

Franciscans vs. Benedictines vs. Dominicans

The Dilemma: Bless me, Father, but I can't tell you guys apart.

People You Can Impress: Gregorian chant fans

The Quick Trick: Franciscans' robes are gray or brown, Dominicans' are white with black cloaks, Benedictines' are usually black but sometimes white.

The Explanation:

Benedictines, oldest of all Catholic monastic orders, follow the order of St. Benedict of Nursia. Writing their Rule in the sixth century, Benedict's precepts had three guidelines: community stability, conversion of manner, and obedience. Further, the abbot of the monastery was considered the father (that's what "abbot" means) and the monks his family. The truth is, any stability to be found in Europe during the Dark Ages came from the Benedictines. But corruption within the order led to a wide-ranging reform in the tenth century centered at the Abbey of Cluny, which brought new organization and vigor. On a slightly different note, the Trappists, who in Belgium make Chimay beer and in Kentucky make cheese, are actually another Benedictine offshoot.

As for the Franciscans, they're a mendicant ("begging") order founded, as you might expect, by St. Francis of Assisi

(1181–1226), the patron saint of animals. Francis took Christ's call to go forth without shoes or staff or money as a literal command, and founded his Ordo Fratrum Minorum (Order of the Friars Minor, or, more literally, "Order of the Little Brothers") in 1209. Best known for their plain robes (they're still called the Greyfriars in some places), they traveled the countryside singing and preaching. Overall, the Rule of St. Francis was simple, based on a vow of poverty. But it wasn't all happy begging and singing. The friars felt the best way to get closer to God was hard work. To this day, some Franciscan friars still wear the traditional hooded woolen robes, rope belts, and sandals. Notable Franciscans include St. Bonaventure, William of Occam (namesake of "Occam's Razor"), and the fictional Friar Tuck. As for Francis himself, he was believed to have miraculously borne the stigmata (the nail and spear wounds of Christ) late in his life.

St. Dominic de Guzmán founded his order around the same time as St. Francis, and he had one main purpose in mind: preaching (their official name is Ordo Praedicatorum, the Order of Preachers). The Dominicans arose at a time when heresies were rife in parts of Europe, and Dominic wanted to return heretics to the fold. Like the Franciscans, the Dominicans were mendicant friars, and they had their own set of precepts: poverty, chastity, and obedience. Despite their godly mission, or perhaps because of it, the Dominicans were the driving force behind the Inquisition. In fact, St. Thomas Aquinas was a Dominican, as was the terrifying Grand Iquisitor, Torquemada.

o o o o o o o o o o

Samurai vs. Ninja

The Dilemma: You've accepted the fact that there's a quartet of high-kicking mutant turtles terrorizing the local sewer system. The real question is: Are these hard-shelled hooligans a bunch of samurai or ninja?

People You Can Impress: If you manage to parlay this information into *becoming* either a ninja or a samurai, you'll impress most everybody.

The Quick Trick: Samurai wore elaborate armor and never stabbed anybody in the back; ninjas wore no armor and *loved* stabbing people in the back.

The Explanation:

The word *samurai* is somewhat analogous to *European knight:* They were considered nobility, worked for noble higher-ups, and were renowned for their great bravery and code of honor. So much so that all the little kids wanted to grow up to be samurai! (Or so we imagine.) Ninja, on the other hand, were well-disguised mercenary assassins governed by no code save secrecy.

The samurai arose in the 10th century, working as a kind of police force for the Japanese city of Kyoto. By the 12th century, the samurai life as we know it today was established; samurai were well-educated men who could read, write, and kill thanks to their extensive martial arts training. They also adhered to the Bushido, an orally transmitted ethical code that forbade samurai from striking enemies from behind or pillaging unnecessarily. It also required them to commit ritual suicide, known as Seppuku, if they dishonored themselves or the samurai tradition.

At the peak of the tradition, between 7 and 10 percent of the Japanese population—most of Japan's army—were considered samurai. And although samurai are usually depicted with swords, they did adapt to modern warfare with firearms in the late 16th century. In fact, samurai helped Japan to win wars against Korea, China, and even Spain, staying on the scene until the end of the 19th century.

If the samurai relied upon a code of honor, the ninja relied upon their stealth and ferocity. Technically, a ninja is anyone who practices the Japanese martial art ninjutsu (meaning that you, too, can become a ninja just by visiting your local neighborhood dojo!). Because *ninjutsu* teaches everything from stick fighting and knife throwing to disguising yourself and predicting the weather, figures like the 16th-century Shogun Tokugawa Ieyasu have employed ninja tactics to escape enemies early in their political careers. But almost from the beginning, the myth of the ninja proved even more compelling than the reality of them. Long before their portrayal in movies, ninjas were romanticized by everyday Japanese citizens, who shared stories of the ninjas flying, or making themselves invisible. The real ninjas, meanwhile, were mostly schlepping about, spying and assassinating, just trying to pay the bills.

Science

o o o o o o o o o o

Grizzly vs. Black Bear

The Dilemma: A fearsome creature that could split your body in two with a few well-aimed swats is standing before you on its hind legs. You, curious intellect that you are, can't help but wonder about this creature's species.

People You Can Impress: everybody—if you survive

The Quick Trick: Grizzlies are brown; black bears are (get this) also sometimes brown—so that may not help. A quick way of telling the difference between the two is: If the bear in question just gored you to death, there's at least a 70 percent chance it was a grizzly.

The Explanation:

Both bear varieties get a bad rap. In the past 100 years, only about 35 black bear–related fatalities have been reported in North America. The purportedly terrifying grizzly, by comparison, has been responsible for perhaps 100 deaths in the past century. The lowly mosquito, meanwhile, kills about 2 million people a year. But while neither bear is much of a man eater, you're significantly better off running into a black bear than a grizzly. Sure, black bears are adept tree climbers, which cuts off a potential escape route. But they're relatively small—adults usually weigh between 150 and 350 pounds. And they're pretty relaxed. Many black bears are so tame that they'll eat food from your hand (although we advise against trying it, because it 1) is illegal, 2) can cause dependence on human food, which is bad for the bears, and 3) also potentially is bad for your hand).

Grizzly bears, meanwhile, don't have such a laid-back reputation. Also known as bruins and brown bears, grizzlies can weigh 1,400 pounds, stand 13 feet tall, run 35 miles per hour, and kill you with a single swat of the paw. While black bears are found throughout North America, grizzlies now live primarily in Alaska and Canada's Yukon Territory. (Both the UCLA Bruins and the Cal–Berkeley Golden Bears have a grizzly mascot, but the bear hasn't been seen in California since 1922.) Grizzlies prefer vegetables to meat, but sustaining 1,400 pounds on a diet of berries ain't easy. To compensate, their favorite protein-rich food is the moth. If you think *you're* scared of bears, imagine the plight of the Alaskan moth: Grizzlies can wolf down as many as 40,000 of them in a single day.

The Grizzly Question

So black and brown bears differ in size, temperament, and habitat. But none of this addresses the real question: Is Yogi Bear a black bear or a grizzly? The most famous resident of Jellystone Park is brown—but, as noted, so are many black bears. Both bears will scavenge for food, leaving pic-a-nic baskets in danger. But since Yogi stood on two legs and is, after all, smarter than the average bear—we feel he is indisputably a grizzly. Grizzlies stand on their hind legs much more often than black bears and also have bigger brains.

○ ○ ○ ○ ○ ○ ○ ○ ○ ○ ○

Amphetamines vs. Methamphetamines

The Dilemma: You've recently been diagnosed with ADHD and are wondering whether or not your doctor has prescribed you crank to treat your hyperactivity. Because while you're not an MD or anything, that seems like a bad idea.

People You Can Impress: This is the rare bit of knowledge you can use to impress both chemists and drug addicts.

The Quick Trick: If you're taking diet pills, that's amphetamine. If you're smoking crystal, that's methamphetamine (and also not so good for you).

The Explanation:

The difference here, we regret to report, involves some polysyllabic chemistry, but on the up side, the periodic table need not be mentioned. Both drugs are stimulants of the central nervous system, just like MDMA, commonly known as Ecstasy. But amphetamine is known technically as methylated phenylethylamine, while methamphetamine is known as *double* methylated phenylethylamine. The second methylation (to make up a word) changes the compound's interaction with the body.

Regular amphetamine can be plenty bad for you. Speed is

found in everything from the ADHD drug Adderall to diet pills. Many nations, including the U.S., also sometimes give amphetamines to members of the armed forces to increase alertness. But it comes with more than a couple problems: First, it's addictive. Second, it can cause heart attacks. Third, it can cause "amphetamine psychosis," which is very similar to schizophrenia except you have more energy. But such side effects are rarely a problem for those who take amphetamines as prescribed.

Methamphetamine, on the other hand, is widely considered too dangerous to be prescribed. Somewhat stronger than an amphetamine, meth was first synthesized by a Japanese scientist in 1919. Widely prescribed in America and abroad in the 1950s, meth was used to treat everything from alcoholism (ironic because, at best, it only caused a switch in addictions) to Parkinson's (ironic because meth causes involuntary body tics). The production of meth, which involves mixing over-the-counter cold medication with hydriodic acid, wasn't even illegal in much of the U.S. until 1986.

Long known as a drug abused mostly by truckers and bikers, meth only spread into the larger population in the 1980s. But by the year 2000, 4 percent of Americans polled acknowledged having used meth at least once. The allure of meth is that it's very cheap and makes you very high—the drug gives you a feeling of ecstasy caused by dopamine flooding the central nervous syndrome. Unfortunately, this eventually leads to irreversible brain damage.

But that's not all. Chronic abuse is associated with paranoia, hallucinations, strokes, and dementia. Also, it is exceptionally bad for your breath. And it's no fun to get off the stuff: Withdrawal symptoms include seizures.

o o o o o o o o o o

Celsius vs. Kelvin

The Dilemma: Your brand-new European thermometer tells you that it's 114 degrees. Or maybe –114. It's hard to tell. And is that hot or cold or what?

People You Can Impress: meteorologists and your Weather Channel–obsessed grandma

The Quick Trick: If the temperature is below 0, it's either Celsius or the laws of physics have changed. If the temperature is over 200, you're either on fire or measuring in Kelvins.

The Explanation:

The Kelvin is the standard metric system unit of temperature, although almost no one ever tells the temperature by saying that it is "17 Kelvins." Incidentally, if it is 17 Kelvins outside, all human life has come to an end. Zero degrees Kelvin is absolute zero, the temperature at which molecular motion stops. (Absolute zero is approximately –459.67 degrees Fahrenheit, or, calculated on the coldheartedness scale, "colder than Joseph Stalin's heart.") Water freezes at 273.15 Kelvin and boils at 373.15.

This makes for some extremely high temperatures, which is *why* no one really uses the Kelvin to tell temperature. Instead, they use Celsius. Celsius is merely Kelvin plus 273.15. Ergo, water freezes at 0 degrees Celsius and boils at 100. Simple, no?

The Kelvin/Celsius method of measuring temperature is much more logical than the Fahrenheit method used in America, perhaps because the Kelvin is based on hard scientific data, while the Fahrenheit is based on one guy's random encounters with nature. Legend has it that the German physicist Daniel Gabriel Fahrenheit picked his temperature scale by making 0 degrees the coldest outdoor temperature he could find in his town, and making 100 degrees the temperature of his own body. If true, Fahrenheit had a low-grade fever when he came up with his totally not user-friendly scale—which would explain a lot.

Some Important Degrees in Fahrenheit

While Celsius and Kelvin have significant events marking their 0 and 100, Fahrenheit is a bit more random:

Fahrenheit 32: the temperature at which water freezes

Fahrenheit 212: the temperature at which water boils

Fahrenheit 451: the temperature at which books burn (according to Ray Bradbury's eponymously titled novel)

Fahrenheit 136: highest temperature ever recorded on Earth (Al Aziziyah, Libya, in September 1922)

Fahrenheit 135: minimum temperature recommended by the FDA for cooking beef and pork roasts

o o o o o o o o o o o

Tropic of Cancer vs. Tropic of Capricorn

The Dilemma: You know they're both very important, albeit completely imaginary, lines. But that's about all you've got.

People You Can Impress: astrologers

The Quick Trick: The Tropic of Cancer is located above the equator; Capricorn, below it.

The Explanation:

There are five major latitudinal circles on earth, and we like to think of them in a clothing metaphor: The Equator, located at 0 degrees latitude, is the earth's belt. The Tropic of Cancer, located at 23 degrees, 26 minutes, 22 seconds north of the Equator, is sort of the Earth's bra. (The Earth, for the purposes of this metaphor, is a lady.) The Tropic of Capricorn, founds 23 degrees, 26 minutes, 22 seconds south of the equator, is the Earth's garter belt. The Arctic Circle (66°33'38"N) is the Earth's choker necklace, while the Earth's socks rise to the Antarctic Circle (66°33'38"S).

We know what you're wondering (aside from why the Earth is apparently not wearing a blouse): How do we know the astrological sign of imaginary lines? Did we get drunk at a bar and sidle up to them and just *ask*? No. The Tropics of Cancer and Capricorn mark the northernmost and southernmost points on the Earth where the sun can be seen directly above (in summer for Cancer and winter for Capricorn). When the latitudinal lines were named hundreds of years ago, the sun was entering the constellations of Cancer and Capricorn during the summer and winter solstices, respectively. But because stars change position relative to the sun over time, the sun is now in Sagittarius during the winter solstice and Taurus during the summer solstice. In short, the Tropics are due for a renaming—but tradition will probably hold; otherwise we might have to rename the Henry Miller novels (see below).

Tropic of Cancer vs. *Tropic of Capricorn*: The Literary Edition

Published in 1934 and 1939, respectively, Henry Miller's erotic novels *Tropic of Cancer* and *Tropic of Capricorn* caused quite a scandal. The publisher of a pirated edition of *Cancer* was imprisoned for 10 years, and both novels were banned for decades in the United States until the Supreme Court affirmed their literary value in 1964. The difference between the two? Both are very, very dirty and star a guy named "Henry Miller," but *Capricorn* is set in New York, while *Cancer* takes place in Miller's adopted hometown, Paris. Also, only *Cancer* was once featured in an episode of *Seinfeld*. (It's the one where Jerry gets a notice from the library that he's had the book checked out since 1971.)

o o o o o o o o o o o

Type 1 vs. Type 2 Diabetes

The Dilemma: Having just finished a six-pack of Mountain Dew, a Pixy Stick the size of a walking cane, and a state fair's worth of cotton candy, you can feel your teeth vibrating. Also, you're vaguely worried you might be at risk for some type of diabetes—but which one?

People You Can Impress: fifth-graders who snort Fun Dip on double-dog dares

The Quick Trick: You may know Type 1 as "juvenile diabetes." If the body is producing any insulin, it's Type 2.

The Explanation:

Technically known as *diabetes mellitus,* diabetes is marked by persistent or recurring elevated levels of blood sugar. Although it can be treated with changes in diet, exercise, and the injection of insulin (more on that in a moment), diabetes is not curable. And untreated it has the potential to escalate pretty quickly. Diabetes can lead to coma, heart disease, kidney failure, blindness, amputation, and even impotence.

Type 1 diabetes has been recognized since time immemorial. Usually beginning in childhood or adolescence, a misfiring autoimmune response within the body starts destroying the pancreatic cells that create insulin, the hormone that removes glucose from the blood. Without insulin, the body suffers twofold: High blood sugar causes damage to the eyes, heart, and other organs, and poor protein synthesis leads to a general weakening of the body. In short, without insulin, you die—which is precisely what happened to all Type 1 diabetics until 1922, when two scientists, Sir Frederick Grant Banting and Charles Best, discovered insulin and its significance. And while Banting and Best could have gotten fabulously rich by patenting their discovery, they chose not to, so that relatively inexpensive insulin therapy could be immediately available worldwide. How wonderfully, amazingly Canadian of them. Ever since, Type 1 diabetes has become a chronic but not necessarily fatal disease—and while it's no fun injecting yourself with insulin every day, it sure beats dying in your teens.

As for Type 2 diabetes, no one knew it existed until 1935, when physician Harry Himsworth identified it. Today approximately 95 percent of diabetes cases in America are Type 2. Sometimes called slow-onset diabetes, Type 2 generally appears over the course of several years. Here the body produces insulin, but cells don't respond to it correctly. The first treatment for Type 2 diabetes is almost always a change in diet, exercise habits, and weight loss. Type 2 diabetes disproportionately affects the sedentary, obese, and elderly. And while it, too, is incurable, it can usually be controlled without insulin therapy.

All in all, you'd rather have Type 2. Type 1 diabetes decreases life expectancy by an average of 15 years, while the average Type 2 diabetic only lives 5 to 10 fewer years than a typical nondiabetic. That said, many diabetics of both types lead long and healthy lives—and Type 1ers owe it all to those selfless Canadians.

o o o o o o o o o o o

Nuclear Bomb vs. Dirty Nuclear Bomb

The Dilemma: *What Just Happened?!?!?!?!?!?!?!?!*
People You Can Impress: fellow survivors
The Quick Trick: If you're standing in an absolute wasteland amid thousands of corpses, it was a nuclear bomb. If you're standing in a normal city street amid a moderate amount of inconvenience, it was a dirty nuclear bomb.

The Explanation:

Here is the primary difference: Nuclear bombs have, in the past 50 years, killed hundreds of thousands of people. Dirty nuclear bombs have, in all of human history, killed exactly no one—partly because they aren't terribly dangerous and partly because not one has ever been detonated.

Conventional nuclear weapons get their explosive power from either nuclear fission or fusion. The bombs dropped on Hiroshima and Nagasaki—the only nuclear weapons that have been used in warfare—were both fission bombs. Fusion bombs, sometimes called hydrogen bombs, are even more powerful—the U.S. once detonated a 15-megaton fusion bomb in a test. That's approximately 100 times more powerful than "Little Boy," the nuclear weapon dropped on Hiroshima that instantly killed 100,000 people. Most modern bombs combine fission and fusion: a small fission bomb is used to create heat adequate to fuel the fusion.

Even with the physics know-how, the bombs require exceedingly rare isotopes of either plutonium or uranium. The process of getting the elements to the necessary isotope is known as enrichment, and enrichment is generally the stumbling block for nations looking to join the nuclear club. It was even a challenge for the U.S.: Almost 90 percent of the Manhattan Project's budget was spent enriching uranium.

In short, nuclear weapons are extremely difficult to make—and we hope they always will be. A dirty nuclear bomb, on the other hand, could be made by a reasonably smart 14-year-old with access to hospital equipment. Dirty bombs combine conventional explosives (say, dynamite) with radioactive materials (say, cesium, which is used in radiation treatment for cancer patients). Almost all scientists believe that even in the case of a well-designed dirty bomb, the explosive would cause much more damage than the radiation. The fact is there just aren't any acquirable materials radioactive enough to cause much fallout. And while it could be very expensive and inconvenient to clean up an urban area after a dirty bomb attack—that's about it. In short, the difference between the two is that conventional nuclear weapons are infinitely more worrisome.

"Dirty" Little Secrets

The only recorded attempt to detonate a dirty bomb came in 1995, when Chechen rebels—who had been on the forefront of terrorism techniques since the Soviet Union's breakup—called reporters to say they'd planted a bomb in a Moscow park. Made of dynamite and cesium taken from a cancer treatment center, the dynamite might have killed people, but its cesium would have been just the equivalent of a few X rays for those walking past the park. Regardless, the bomb was defused before it exploded.

o o o o o o o o o o o

El Niño vs. La Niña

The Dilemma: You just lost your house in a mud slide, and you need to know precisely what to curse. Mainly, because it's not very dramatic when you raise your fist to the sky and shout, "Darn you, El Niño! Or possibly La Niña!"

People You Can Impress: that gorgeous reporter from the Weather Channel you've been secretly stalking for years, from hurricane to typhoon and back again

The Quick Trick: *El niño* means "little boy"; *la niña,* "little girl." Knowing that, all you have to remember is that little boys are much less sugar, spice, and everything nice than little girls.

The Explanation:

Both El Niño and La Niña are abnormal ocean temperatures in the eastern Pacific Ocean, off the coast of South America. El Niños, wherein the ocean temperature rises at least .5 degree Celsius above normal, occur every two to seven years. An El Niño may or may not be followed by a La Niña, which is basically El Niño's opposite. La Niñas involve colder-than-usual ocean water in the eastern Pacific. An El Niño ended in the spring of 2005; the last significant La Niña was in the fall of 2000.

So who cares if the temperature of the ocean goes up or down a little? Well, most everyone on the planet, as it turns out. The unusually strong tantrums thrown by a one-two El

Niño/La Niña punch in 1997 and 1998 alerted the world to the impacts of very slight oceanic temperature changes. El Niño alone is believed responsible for more than 2,000 deaths from flooding, mud slides, and storms. It's also estimated to have cost $33 billion in property damage—more than Hurricane Katrina. While the worst effects were seen in South America, the warm water fed thunderstorms that spread around the world, flooding rivers from Poland to Chile. Much of Indonesia, on the other hand, experienced drought. (El Niño did, however, make for a pleasantly warm winter for those of us living in the northern United States. Ah, silver linings.) La Niña also wreaked havoc on world climate in 1998, but far less dramatically.

Scientists disagree about what causes these weather phenomena. Some say it has to do with increases in the Western trade winds; others believe the water temperature heats up for several years near the equator before it spreads out to sea.

Too Much Pressure: Low vs. High Pressure Systems

So what are TV meteorologists talking about when they vaguely wave their hand over a huge swathe of the map and insist that there's a "low" or "high" pressure system in the area? Basically, low pressure systems—i.e., areas of unusually low air pressure—are associated with precipitation (including everything from rain showers to category 5 hurricanes). The lower the air pressure, generally, the stronger the storm. High pressure systems, meanwhile, usually portend sunny skies and cooler temperatures. This is why winter days tend to be colder when it's sunny (high pressure) rather than cloudy (lower pressure).

o o o o o o o o o o

Bee vs. Hornet vs. Wasp

The Dilemma: "What just stung me?!"
People You Can Impress: six-year-olds, maybe
The Quick Trick: A bee can generally only sting you once, while hornets and wasps can sting multiple times.

The Explanation:

The problem with elucidating the difference between wasps and hornets is that, at least according to most definitions of wasps, *all* hornets are wasps. So here's the deal:

Bees are fuzzy pollen collectors that almost always die shortly after stinging people (because the stinger becomes embedded in the skin, which prevents multiple stings). Bees don't die *each time* they sting, though; the primary purpose of the stinger is to sting other bees, which doesn't result in the loss of the stinger.

Wasps are members of the family Vespidae, which includes yellow jackets and hornets. Wasps generally have two pairs of wings and are definitely not fuzzy. Only the females have stingers, but they can sting people repeatedly.

Hornets are a small subset of wasps not native to North America (the yellow jacket is not truly a hornet). Somewhat fatter around the middle than your average wasp, the European hornet is now widespread on the East Coast of the U.S.

Like other wasps, hornets can sting over and over again and can be extremely aggressive.

The Best Darn Animal Roundup Since Noah!

Monarch Butterfly vs. Viceroy Butterfly: Both butterflies have very similar bright orange markings and excrete a bitter acid that makes them taste terrible. But only the monarch flies thousands of miles south in the winter.

Snail vs. Slug: Snails have telltale spiral shells; slugs have shells, too, but they're invisible because they're located inside their bodies.

Donkey vs. Mule: A mule is the offspring of a female horse (that is, a mare) and a jackass (that is, either a male donkey or Johnny Knoxville). Mules are sterile and slow, but they're also strong and hard-working. A donkey is an animal closely related to the horse (obviously, since they can mate), but donkeys are smaller and have longer ears. (See also Eeyore.)

Llama vs. Emu: Both are newly domesticated farm animals, but that's where the similarity ends: Llamas belong to the camel family, while emus are birds related to ostriches. But the two animals do have one thing in common: crankiness. When llamas get annoyed, which is frequently, they spit up their own stomach acid. And emus are largely solitary animals that don't like too much human company.

Mighty Mouse vs. Mickey Mouse: Mickey was created in the 1920s by Walt Disney, while Mighty (a Terrytoons character) wasn't born until 1942. Mickey has no superpowers, while Mighty is excellent at flying and has X-ray vision.

o o o o o o o o o o o

Clones vs. Originals

The Dilemma: Your kid and the clone he just created emerge from the basement "lab" looking exactly the same, and now you're not sure which one to ship off to military school and which one to put up for adoption.

People You Can Impress: anyone who likes puzzles

The Quick Trick: Find out their ages. The clone will be seconds, minutes, days, or years younger. Also, if you're willing to wait it out, you'll find clones tend to die faster.

The Explanation:

Clones are basically organisms that have been created from a single individual through asexual reproduction. In the recent past, sheep (like the infamous Dolly), mice, cows, kittens, and dogs have all been cloned, much to the chagrin of ethicists and religious leaders around the globe. In fact, the looming possibility of human cloning has added urgency to their platform.

While the genetic makeup of a clone and its original are almost entirely identical (with less than 1 percent discrepancy between their genetic codes), clones don't always look exactly like their originals. Cloned dairy cows, for instance, may have spots in different locations and slightly different personalities—perhaps because they come out of separate uterine environments.

Scientists don't have a good understanding of why clones

tend to age prematurely and die young. Dolly the sheep, for instance, developed arthritis when she was just 2, and died at 6 of a lung disease extremely rare in young sheep, whereas the life expectancy of a sheep is about 12. The problem may be that having an identical genetic makeup doesn't mean that all those genes will be *expressed* identically, and clones may not be able to express genes as effectively. But all this talk of expressing genes leads us to Express Jeans. . . .

It's in the Jeans

Anyone who's purchased jeans in the past decade has no doubt noted the price inflation. But the world's most expensive jeans? Those would be the tricked-out blue jeans from APO, which have a diamond-studded main button and rivets of precious metals (somewhere Levi Strauss must be rolling in his grave) and cost *$4,000!*

Rael Problems in Cloning

The Raelian Movement (which got its start when a guy named Rael Claude Vorilhon self-published a book called *The Message Given to Me by Extra-Terrestrials*) believes that really smart space aliens created life on earth through genetic engineering. Rael also prophesied way back in the mid-1970s that human cloning would prove to be the key to immortality. Perhaps that's why a Raelian-funded corporation, Clonaid, announced on December 26, 2002, that a cloned baby had just been born. However, the group has consistently refused to let anyone see this purported "baby," and pretty much everyone agrees the "cloning" was a hoax. However, the Raelians sue every publication that points out the ridiculousness of their cloning claims, so we'd just like to go on record saying that we're sure the Raelians probably *have* cloned a baby and certainly aren't *completely nuts!*

o o o o o o o o o o o

Blimp vs. Zeppelin

The Dilemma: You're at a football game and there's a large, cigar-shaped object hovering suspiciously close to you. Question: Is it a blimp or a zeppelin? And more important, why didn't you get better seats?

People You Can Impress: whoever's perched in the nosebleeds next to you

The Quick Trick: When in doubt, just think of Led Zeppelin. Zeppelins are heavy metal—or at least they've got metal skeletons. Blimps, on the other hand, aren't.

The Explanation:

Both blimps and zeppelins work by being lighter than air—they're filled with a gas that's lighter than oxygen, so they go up like hot-air balloons. But balloons can't be steered. Realizing this, German Count (Graf) Ferdinand von Zeppelin decided he wanted to devise a "dirigible [or steerable] balloon" in the 1890s for use in the military reconnaissance work. Eventually, these dirigible balloons took the generic name zeppelin and were used as bombers or scout craft through World War I. This was just one of their many uses, however. The airships doubled as a major mode of transportation between the wars, routinely making transatlantic flights, and the enormous *Graf Zeppelin* even circumnavigated the globe in 1929.

So just how popular were these zeppelins? Well, enough that the spire on the top of the Empire State Building was designed as a docking mast for them, although that idea proved impractical due to the serious updrafts (and besides, who wants to disembark while dangling 1,300 feet over Manhattan?).

Incidentally, anyone who's seen the footage of the *Hindenburg* incinerating at Lakehurst, N.J. in 1937 can see evidence of the main difference between zeppelins and blimps: zeppelins have rigid metal skeletons, making them suitable for longer trips in a wider variety of weather conditions (which also makes them expensive). Blimps, on the other hand, are simply shaped balloons with fins and an engine. Oh, and as for the name "blimp"? It dates back to 1916 and mimics the sound made when the balloon is thumped with a finger.

Led and Other Zeppelins

Led Zeppelin is to date the greatest band ever named after a flying machine (take that, Jefferson Airplane). And while their sound is pretty original, the band's name is completely attributable to Keith Moon, the late and eccentric drummer of The Who. The pessimistic Moon thought the band, originally called the New Yardbirds, would "go over like a lead zeppelin." But the plucky young band reveled in the challenge and quickly adopted the name—with a minor change in spelling.

Frogs vs. Toads

The Dilemma: You just kissed an amphibian that *ribbits*. Will it turn into a prince, or will you hallucinate? And do they both taste like chicken?

People You Can Impress: herpetologists, lonely princesses, and Miss Piggy

The Quick Trick: The wartier the skin, the more likely it's a toad.

The Explanation:

First, let's discuss how to generally tell the two apart (this isn't completely foolproof). To begin with, toads' bodies tend to be shorter and wider while frogs' are thinner and sleeker. Toads also spend less time in water than frogs, so—side by side—a frog's feet appear more webbed than its warty cousin's. Toads also have two bumps on their heads, the parotid glands, which they can use to secrete poison. Frogs, on the other hand, have generally longer legs and are better jumpers. Plus, they tend to be wetter, shinier, and smoother than the dry-skinned toad.

In terms of self-defense, toads (and a few frogs) tend to protect themselves from predators by secreting various toxins from their skins, which in small doses can have interesting results. Ingest the venom of the *Bufo alvarius,* and you'll trip out. However, take in the venom of the Amazonian poison dart frog, and you'll be having a chat with St. Peter in no time.

The one kind of toad that most Americans can name (and

giggle when they do) is the erroneously called horny toad. Others (notably those at Texas Christian University, where it's their mascot) call the animal the horned *frog*. Strangely enough, both are wrong. The creature is neither a toad nor a frog. In fact, it's not even an amphibian! It's a lizard.

Toads Gone Wild

Toads aren't native to Australia. But Australians sure have more than they know what to do with. So how'd it come to be? The cane toad is the Down Under's equivalent of kudzu: an introduced species that ran amok. In 1935, 101 cane toads were brought to Australia in the hope of protecting sugarcane from pests. Without any predators, though, the toads went bananas. In fact, today there are so many toads that they're starting to mess up the whole ecosystem.

How the French Became Frogs

We'd be remiss if we didn't take this opportunity to explain how the term "frog" became a derogatory nickname for the French. Basically, it boils down to three reasons:

1) Both words start with *fr,* and that's just easy;

2) The French eat frogs (particularly their legs) as a delicacy, so "frogs" was probably shortened from "frog-eaters";

3) Some believe that the fleur-de-lis, the heraldic symbol of France (and of the New Orleans Saints) was derived from three toads on the coat of arms of Clovis, king of the Franks, in the fifth century. At the time, toads were thought to represent Satan, so toads on his coat became a *non-non* once the good king converted to Christianity. Thus he quickly replaced them with a representation of the lily, now called the fleur-de-lis.

o o o o o o o o o o

Asian vs. African Elephant

The Dilemma: Something big and gray just crushed your car and stole your peanuts. So what do you tell the insurance company—African elephant or Asian?

People You Can Impress: ringmasters, Carthaginian generals, and members of the GOP

The Quick Trick: The Asian ones are smaller.

The Explanation:

If you're thinking about the typical elephant, the one used to represent Republicans in political cartoons (huge, with great big ears and long, curved tusks), the elephant you're probably picturing is the African elephant, the largest land mammal in the world. More specifically, this most attractive of elephants is the savanna, or bush elephant, one of two separate species in Africa. The other, the forest elephant, can be easily spotted from its larger cousin thanks to its slightly smaller, more rounded ears (the savanna's are pointier), longer, narrower lower jaw, and straight, pinkish tusks. Oddly enough, from a DNA point of view, the forest elephant is actually more similar to the Asian elephant than to its continental counterparts. Frankly, forest elephants got a little shafted by natural selection—their heads seem too small for their bodies.

Asian elephants, on the other hand, used to be called Indian elephants. That is, until the world realized that the elephant species could be found in other parts of the continent as well.

More specifically, Indian elephants are one of four Asian subspecies, along with Borneo, Sumatran, and Sri Lankan elephants (Indian elephants are the most widely domesticated and docile—as far as that goes). As for distinguishing features, you can tell an Asian elephant by its smaller size and more rounded back, the single fingerlike extension on its trunk (Africans have two), the two humps on its head, and—if you care to make a very close inspection—19 pairs of ribs, two pairs fewer than African species (though the Sumatran has 20). Also, if you're a female Asian elephant, no tusks for you.

Ear Conditioning

Believe it or not, an elephant's ears are pretty effective at cooling the animal down. While elephants can use the great flaps to fan themselves, scientists speculate the cooling mechanism is actually much more sophisticated. Elephant ears are packed with blood vessels, are very thin, and have very little insulating fat. As blood passes through an elephant's ears, it's cooled by the air (aided by the fanning of the ears), thereby cooling the entire animal down. So if you think about it, the hotter, drier climate and the larger size of African elephants led them to evolve larger ears.

Good to Know

So which one did Hannibal bring across the Alps to surprise the bejesus out of the Romans? Neither, technically. Hannibal's pachyderms were believed to be North African elephants, an extinct subspecies of African elephant.

As for the word *pachyderm,* it comes from Greek and means "thick skin." While most people use this word as a synonym for elephant, hippopotamuses and rhinoceroses can also accurately be called pachyderms.

o o o o o o o o o o

Meteor vs. Meteorite vs. Meteoroid

The Dilemma: Something from the heavens just crushed your boss, and you're pretty sure it wasn't a foul ball.

People You Can Impress: astronomers or just folks wishing on "shooting stars"

The Quick Trick: *Oids* are *outside* the atmosphere, *ites* are *inside* it, and meteors are in between.

The Explanation:

Say you're a bit of interplanetary dust or debris trucking through the vacuum of space, minding your own business. You're not very big. Certainly not big enough to be called an asteroid. In fact, you might just be a speck of dust or even smaller. Congrats! You're a *meteoroid*!

But say, for example, a bright blue planet suddenly gets in your way and sucks you in, and before you know it you're streaking through an atmosphere so fast that you *ablate* (fancy way to say "vaporize") and let off a bright streak of light. You are now officially a *meteor*.

Now, on the other hand, if you started out big enough, then enough of you will emerge from this furnace o' friction to hit the ground in some farmer's field, making you a *meteorite*. Mazel tov! Of course, we should specify here: If you're made of rock, you're called a *chondrite*. Mostly metal? You're an *iron meteorite*. A little of both? Say, a rock wrapped in metal? You are hereby dubbed a *pallasite*.

Believe it or not, about 25 million meteoroids hit Earth's atmosphere every day. And while most of them burn away to nothing, sometimes the Earth's orbit will take them through a messy patch of interplanetary junk, like the orbit of a dead comet that's broken into millions of meteoroids. In such a case, the Earth's gravity can hoover up these particles by the millions—creating meteor showers. A huge shower emanates from the direction of the constellation Perseus every August, for instance, creating an event that's widely publicized and not to be missed.

So What's an Asteroid?

Just as meteoroids are too small to be called asteroids, asteroids are too small to be called planets. Most asteroids that have been discovered (there are now well over 100,000) range from about 10 kilometers to 100 kilometers in diameter and are found in a belt between Mars and Jupiter. In fact, scientists believe that this asteroid belt was a nascent planet that, bullied by Jupiter's immense gravity, never quite got it together.

Asteroids are grouped into a number of families based on their orbits. Those whose orbits cross the Earth's orbits are called Apollo asteroids. Earth crossing is not a good thing, however. If an asteroid just 1 kilometer across were to hit the Earth, we wouldn't get a pretty light show. We'd get a jolt equivalent to a 20-megaton nuclear blast, leaving a crater with a diameter equal to the length of Manhattan. That kind of jolt is survivable—if you're a character in the movie *Deep Impact*. If you're a human on earth, it stirs up a bit more trouble.

o o o o o o o o o o

Neanderthal vs. Cro-Magnon

The Dilemma: At a cocktail party, a nasty brute spills a drink on you. You'd like to compare his manners to that of a more primitive hominid. But which would be more insulting?

People You Can Impress: Anthropologists—they're just happy to talk to someone who's not a fossilized skeletal fragment.

The Quick Trick: Neanderthals are more primitive but stronger. Cro-Magnons are us.

The Explanation:

Cognitively speaking, it's definitely more insulting to call someone a Neanderthal. But if you're talking musculature, they might just take it as a compliment. Neanderthals (*Homo neanderthalensis*) were discovered first in Germany's Neander Valley in 1856. They emerged between 100,000 and 200,000 years ago, give or take, in the early and middle Paleolithic era, and they used tools, albeit very simple ones. Often they resorted to using rocks (or flakes broken off of rocks by hitting them with other rocks), bones, and sticks. And they used fire, too! Neanderthals were more muscular than the later Homo sapiens, and their skulls were flatter, with broad noses and pronounced ridges on the forehead (which is why, to us, they look rather dim). They were also capable of speech, but recent physiological discoveries indicate that their voices were high pitched and nasal, not the baritone grunts we normally associate with cavemen. Despite their similarities to us, they were not—repeat, *not*—a step on the way to us. They were a dead-end offshoot of an earlier common ancestor, and they eventually lost out to their smarter, more advanced cousins: Cro-Magnons.

As for Cro-Magnons, they're pretty much just like us. They take their name from a cave in France where Louis Lartet found them in 1868 (well, he found their skeletons. They had died a while before). Unlike Neanderthals, Cro-Magnons are *not* a separate species from *Homo sapiens*. In fact, they're the earliest known European example of *our species*—living between 35,000 and 10,000 years ago—and are actually modern in every anatomical respect. They did, however, have somewhat broader faces, a bit more muscle, and a *slightly* larger brain. So how'd they utilize their larger noggins? Cro-Magnon man used tools, spoke and probably sang, made weapons, lived in huts, wove cloth, wore skins, made jewelry, used burial rituals, made cave paintings, and even came up with a calendar. Specimens have since been found outside Europe, including in the Middle East.

Amazingly, the two species actually overlapped in Europe for a few thousand years. So did they interbreed? While scientists allow that there were probably plenty of random matings and hookups, any long-term interbreeding is unlikely. And while there are many reasons for this, the simplest are that a) they were probably physically repulsive to each other, and b) they couldn't meaningfully communicate. And also c) beer wasn't invented yet.

o o o o o o o o o o

Quasar vs. Pulsar

The Dilemma: You boned up all night on Miss Cleo and star signs only to find out her passion's actually *astronomy*.

People You Can Impress: astrophysicists, astronomers, and Jodie Foster's character in the movie *Contact*

The Quick Trick: Pulsars are *pulsing* stars. Quasars are *quasi*-stars.

The Explanation:

When a huge star goes supernova, it collapses into a dense, dark neutron star. This thing is pretty odd—a small star that's about as big across as the length of Manhattan, but more massive than the sun. They're too massive to be a white dwarf (a threshold of 1.4 times our sun's mass), but not massive enough to be a black hole.

The pulsar, a rapidly spinning neutron star, was discovered in 1967 by Antony Hewish and Jocelyn Bell. Together the pair detected electromagnetic radiation being "broadcast" at regular intervals, which they believed might have been signals from aliens. Their half-serious theory of "little green men" spurred them to jokingly dub their discovery LGM-1. It now goes by the more appropriately sedate designation PSR 1919+21 (that means it's a pulsar located at right ascension of 19 hours, 19 minutes, and 21 degrees declination. Astronomers, you see, do not like the funny).

Pulsars are so called because they "pulse" with emissions at a steady rate. For example, PSR 1919 + 21 pulses every 1.337 seconds. Of course, there are several varieties, but the most common are rotation powered. These pulsars rotate incredibly fast, throwing off beams of radio waves or X-rays from their magnetic poles. Like a lighthouse, which to a distant observer would appear to "pulse," pulsars only *appear* to pulse. We only see the light when the beam points our way.

Quasars also emit radio waves and radiation but are not technically stars. They're said to be starlike because they emit light. In fact, they are the brightest objects in the universe, more luminous than several thousand galaxies put together. So why aren't they that bright from where we're sitting? And more important, how did they go undetected until the 1950s? Well, the answer is that they're just too old, meaning they were a feature of the earlier universe. Remember, the farther away something is in the universe, the older it is, because the light takes so long to get here. Plus, they're moving away from us at an amazing clip.

Today eggheads are still arguing about what quasars actually are. Some say they are a type of galaxy formed around a supermassive black hole. Some even believe that our galaxy was once a quasar. If that's the case, all you parents out there worried that your lil' galaxy might be a quasar, relax. It's just a phase.

Regular Gasoline vs. Diesel

The Dilemma: Gas prices have you seriously considering those high-mileage cars with "D" after their names. So what's the difference?

People You Can Impress: gearheads, throttle jockeys, grease monkeys, and even tree huggers!

The Quick Trick: The one that smells like rotten eggs is diesel.

The Explanation:

Start with some of the good stuff. The crude oil. The black gold. The Texas . . . well, you get the picture. At the refinery, the crude oil undergoes a process called fractional distillation, which separates the various compounds in the crude oil based on their different boiling points. The first to go are the flammable gases like propane; while bitumen (the goopy stuff used to tar roads) is the last, boiling off at the highest temperature. In between, however, are things like kerosene, butane, diesel, and gasoline (diesel boils off between 250° and 350°C, gasoline boils around 150°, and kerosene is in between the two).

Gasoline is actually a combination of several products of the refinery. By adjusting the ratios, you get different "grades" of gasoline (regular, super, ultra-high-test, etc.). In fact, one of the numbers you may have noticed on the pump is an "octane rating." Octane is a hydrocarbon found in gasoline that lowers the tendency to prematurely detonate (we hear it happens to a lot of fuels), known as knocking. In technical terms, an 89-octane gasoline has the knock resistance of a mixture of 89 percent isooctane and 11 percent heptane. The short version: Higher is better.

For decades, lead was added to reduce knocking. But then we figured out that lead is really, really bad for you. Nowadays additives like ethanol have taken its place, which is why you don't have to make the "regular or unleaded" choice at the pump anymore.

As for diesel fuel, it has plenty of positives and negatives. The fact is it's almost 20 percent more efficient than gasoline, producing more energy per unit of volume. But it's also much dirtier, with a higher sulfur content (hence that "diesel smell"), and it can produce soot. Luckily, the diesel used all over Europe is cleaner and ignites better than American diesel, partly from stricter environmental controls. The U.S., however, is following suit and will soon be lowering emissions through ultra-low-sulfur diesel.

In terms of the word itself, *diesel* comes from the name of the German engineer Rudolf "No Relation to Vin" Diesel. Rudolf invented an internal combustion engine in 1890 that became known as the diesel engine. Whereas in a regular gasoline engine the gas is ignited by the sparks from spark plugs, diesels are compression-ignited engines, meaning that the fuel ignites when mixed with high-temperature, high-pressure air. It's this rapid intake exhaust of air that gives the diesel its characteristic "chugga-chugga" sound.

TNT vs. Dynamite

The Dilemma: Either you're a rabid AC/DC fan in search of lyrical meaning or you've got some pressing need to blow something up. Either way, we've got your answer.

People You Can Impress: demolition experts, mustachioed villains from silent movies, and Wile E. Coyote

The Quick Trick: If it's a white powder found in sticks, it's dynamite. If it's a yellow crystal, it's TNT. Use this little mnemonic to remember dynamite's inventor: "Winning a Nobel Prize would be *dynamite!*" The alternative, that winning would be TNT, just doesn't make any sense.

The Explanation:

A lot of people use these two terms interchangeably, and the common misperception is that TNT is the chemical name and dynamite is the colloquial term. But like any good misperception, that's just plain wrong.

We'll start with dynamite. Patented in 1867 by the Swedish chemist Alfred Nobel (as in Nobel Prize), dynamite was discovered when old Alfie was looking for a way to make nitroglycerin more stable and less prone to, well, exploding in your face. By combining nitroglycerine with diatomaceous earth (the ground-up shells of microscopic diatoms, today used as a filtering agent in swimming pools) and sodium carbonate (found in baking soda and soaps), Nobel took explosives in a whole new direction. And because it was stable and wouldn't explode from jiggling, like nitroglycerin, dynamite was initially marketed as Nobel's Safety Blasting Powder. (Well, it wasn't *that* safe; an explosion at the family factory killed Alfred's brother Emil.) Nobel used the huge profits from his dynamite patent to endow the Nobel prizes, one of which is, ironically, for peace.

As for TNT, it's also a high explosive, but it ain't dynamite. TNT is a yellowish compound with the chemical name trinitrotoluene (try-night-row-TALL-you-een), which is somewhat easier to remember than its chemical formula, $CH_3C_6H_2(NO_2)_3$. TNT was discovered in Germany in 1863 by Joseph Wilbrand. Although not quite as powerful as dynamite (and harder to detonate), the main benefit of TNT is that it's even more stable than dynamite (Wilbrand, for instance, never lost a single brother to an explosion). Also, TNT can be melted down and poured into shell casings. On the downside, however, TNT is extremely toxic.

While TNT packs plenty of bang by itself, it's often mixed with other things. A TNT and ammonium nitrate cocktail will get you amatol, a military explosive. Remix those two and add some powdered aluminum, and you'll get ammonal, a common industrial explosive.

AC/DC

The confusion between TNT and dynamite isn't helped by popular culture. The two are routinely used interchangeably in movies. And in the song "TNT" by AC/DC, deceased lead singer Bonn Scott declares "I'm TNT, I'm dynamite." So which one is it, Bonn?

Fission vs. Fusion

The Dilemma: For reasons that are really none of our business, you're extremely curious about nuclear reactions. Hey, that's cool. We're here to help.

People You Can Impress: nuclear physicists, environmental protesters, and just by correctly pronouncing NEW-clee-er, some American presidents

The Quick Trick: Fusion *fuses* elements lighter than iron. Fission *divides* elements heavier than iron.

The Explanation:

These two forms of reaction are called nuclear because the big stuff (that's a technical term) all happens inside the nucleus of an atom.

Let's put it in the simplest terms: Fusion works by smashing atomic nuclei together to create heavier nuclei. In order to make this happen, you have to heat things up a bit—say, a few million degrees Celsius. Fusion is promising as an energy source (and potentially dangerous) because it's exothermic—it produces more energy than it requires to start it and is therefore self-sustaining. How much energy can fusion produce? Well, our sun's been working for several billion years just fine on fusion.

Fusion is difficult to achieve because of something called the coulomb barrier. This is the energy required to overcome the electrostatic force that repells two nuclei from each other.

What makes fusion tricky is that the best fuels, the ones with the lowest coulomb barriers, are the least stable. They are isotopes of hydrogen—deuterium (^{2}H) and tritium (^{3}H)—so named because they have two and three neutrons in their nuclei, respectively. We are not yet able to create a fusion reaction and contain it to use as energy. In fact, the ones we've created that aren't contained are called hydrogen bombs. This has physicists looking for an alternative that requires much less energy to start and contains the Holy Grail of nuclear science known as "cold fusion."

Fission, on the other hand, is the complete opposite: Very large nuclei are split to make smaller ones, releasing energy (and a boatload of radiation) in the process. Again, the best fuels are the most unstable: Isotopes like uranium-235 or plutonium-239 don't occur naturally. Fission is used both for nuclear power plants and nuclear bombs.

To get fission going, you bombard the nucleus with a free particle, like a neutron or photon. The nucleus splits, releasing energy and more neutrons. If the split produces enough neutrons to keep the reaction going, it increases exponentially, and you reach critical mass.

Cold, Hard Facts

In 1989, two researchers at the University of Utah held a press conference and made a stunning announcement: They'd achieved nuclear fusion at room temperature, which offered the promise of an endless supply of cheap energy to the entire world. One problem: The two researchers had actually, as it turns out, not achieved fusion at room temperature. They hadn't achieved it at all. In the years since, neither the original duo (who still claim the announcement wasn't a hoax) nor other researchers have managed to replicate the initial results.

Art, Band, P.E.

FM vs. AM

The Dilemma: As far as you know, the only difference between the two is that AM has more preachers.

People You Can Impress: Those preachers, for starters

The Quick Trick: Static is key. If there's static, it's AM. Of course, that whole thing about the preachers isn't a bad rule of thumb either.

The Explanation:

FM stands for "frequency modulation" and AM stands for "amplitude modulation," so it's not hard to figure out that the distinction is based on the way a radio wave modulates, or fluctuates. FM waves differ from one another based on frequency, or how many times per second the wave's current changes direction. AM waves, however, fluctuate based on amplitude, which refers to the specific strength of the signal. All radio waves experience changes in amplitude as they travel, but obviously, if the amplitude isn't strong enough when it reaches a receiver, you'll hear static. And because AM waves depend on specific amplitudes to get a signal, they're less reliable. This also makes them less valuable, which is why it's easier for all those farm news enthusiasts and mariachi bands to get one of their own.

If you're wondering about their order, there's no chicken and egg here: The AM definitely came first. Inventor Reginald

Fessenden made the first AM radio broadcast in 1906—presaging those radio preachers by making his first broadcast a reading from the Bible and a live performance of himself playing "O Holy Night" on the violin. And while the medium was most popular from 1920 to the advent of FM in the '50s, AM certainly has its limitations. For one thing, AM travels by sound waves close to the Earth during the day and higher in the sky in the evening, meaning it's hard to have a large broadcast radius during daylight hours. For another thing, AM signals, unlike FM, are often disrupted by tall buildings—a bigger problem today than in 1920.

As for FM, it was invented in 1933 by Edwin Armstrong—but sadly enough, Armstrong never lived to see his invention succeed. Convinced FM had failed, Armstrong committed suicide by jumping out of his window in 1954. Just a few years later, the superior sound quality and general betterness of FM were recognized by the American public, and FM took off, making Armstrong's widow rich.

Popularity Contest

FM has supplanted AM as the most popular worldwide format—if you trust the CIA's fact-gathering abilities. According to the CIA's *World Factbook,* there are about 28,693 FM radio stations in the world and only 16,265 AM stations.

o o o o o o o o o o

Bluegrass vs. Country

The Dilemma: You want to expand your musical knowledge, but your eyes glaze over at the mere mention of broken-down trucks and errant wives.

People You Can Impress: fans of both country *and* western

The Quick Trick: Check and see what the musician is packing. Country music generally involves a heavy guitar sound (acoustic and/or electric). If you're going to play bluegrass, though, you'll need a fiddle, a mandolin, or a banjo—and preferably all three.

The Explanation:

Bluegrass and country (to a lesser extent) are both descendants of Appalachian folk music, which remained largely unchanged from the 18th century until the 1920s, when mountain musicians began flocking to cities and were influenced by other popular styles. The recording industry referred to the resulting mix of folk ballads, blues, and gospel as "hillbilly music"—a name it tactfully dropped in favor of "country" in 1949.

By that point, though, a lot of people felt country music had drifted too far from its roots. In the late 1940s, a band called The Blue Grass Boys, fronted by Bill Monroe, led a return to folk standards and traditional instruments such as the fiddle, mandolin, and banjo. Monroe, who is universally regarded as having invented bluegrass music and is talked about in hushed, reverent tones by bluegrass musicians everywhere, was influenced both by the traditional music played by his uncles and by African American folk music of the South.

Since the emergence of Bill Monroe, country and bluegrass have had wildly different trajectories. Country music adopted influences from the tunes of the Western United States and became a multibillion-dollar industry based on guitar melodies, fusion with other popular styles, and slick production values. Meanwhile, bluegrass became the underground music of traditionalists, the 1960s folk scene, and rockers in search of their roots.

But there has certainly been some crossover between bluegrass and the wider world of pop country music. Monroe is in the Country Music Hall of Fame, after all—*and* the Rock and Roll Hall of Fame. And before the Dixie Chicks became the richest women in country, they were a banjo-pickin', foot-thumpin' bluegrass trio.

There's No Tear in *My* Beer

Although known today as the semiofficial musical medium of sentimentality, country once had a different reputation. In fact, the style became all the rage in the 1920s in part because it was *less* maudlin than other popular music.

o o o o o o o o o o

Bach vs. Beethoven

The Dilemma: You asked your dad to "turn that crap down," and he asked you to be more specific.

People You Can Impress: NPR listeners. Perhaps also Dad.

The Quick Trick: Listen for a piano. If you hear it as a prominent instrument in the piece, it's probably by Beethoven.

The Explanation:

Ludwig van Beethoven (1770–1827), generally classified as a Classical composer, wasn't even born until 20 years after Bach had died. Little Ludwig started young on the piano, and the talented tyke was paraded around town by his overbearing father. Beethoven's love for the piano heavily influenced his composition in later years, when he experimented with a number of new pianistic effects, such as the pedal and the use of register extremes. Very popular among the aristocracy in Vienna, Beethoven's works were well appreciated during his lifetime. And although he began to go deaf in 1801, he continued performing and composing until 1817, when his hearing was completely gone.

Bach (1685–1750), usually categorized as a Baroque composer, didn't enjoy nearly the kind of success that Beethoven did during his lifetime. Bach was known more as an organist than as a composer, and although he landed a prestigious gig in 1723 (music director of Leipzig's St. Thomas Church), almost none of his compositions were published during his lifetime. But he composed *tons* of organ music, as well as the occasional violin sonata. While Beethoven's work was largely secular, the majority of Bach's compositions were to be played in church (makes sense, since he worked in one). Bach's use of counterpoint, the sounding of separate lines simultaneously, gave his compositions a layered, robust quality, and by using the full range of keys possible, he revolutionized the organ as a musical instrument. Despite his indisputable brilliance, Bach was largely forgotten for almost 100 years after his death, but in the 19th century his genius began to be recognized by Romantic composers like Felix Mendelssohn, who helped revive Bach's reputation.

Moonlight Sonatas

Beethoven may have had more worldly success, but Bach had a *lot* more mojo than Beethoven. Bach had a total of 20 children: seven from his marriage with his cousin, Maria Barbara Bach, and the other 13 with his second wife, Anna Magdalena Walken. Beethoven, on the other hand, never married. How could a wealthy musician not manage to find a mate? Well, for starters, he wasn't wealthy—he always had trouble keeping track of his finances. Also, he was really, really dirty. He was often seen walking the streets of Vienna wearing filthy rags, muttering to himself. The strange behavior might be attributable, believe it or not, to lead poisoning. Samples from Beethoven's hair tested in 2004 proved that he probably died of lead poisoning, which can cause brain damage.

Symphony vs. Orchestra vs. Philharmonic

The Dilemma: So are the musicians where you've been dragged part of an orchestra, a symphony, or a philharmonic? And more important, is it intermission yet?

People You Can Impress: guys named Ludwig, Wolfgang, or Dmitri

The Quick Trick: All symphonies are orchestras, but only the big orchestras are symphonies.

The Explanation:

Start with the most basic: an orchestra. While the meaning of that word has drifted somewhat over the centuries, today *orchestra* is used to describe a musical group that includes a wind, percussion, and string section—specifically violins, violas, cellos, and basses. If there are no strings, it's a band (or a band with a fancy name, like *wind symphony* or *concert band* or Coldplay). If the orchestra is small—say, fewer than 40 members or even as small as four or five—it's a *chamber orchestra* (because it was once small enough to fit in a chamber, or room, instead of needing a huge concert hall).

There's a point at which an orchestra becomes a symphony orchestra, or just symphony, for short. This distinction has less to do with numbers and more to do with instrumentation.

Symphony orchestras have four sections of instruments: strings, woodwinds, brass, and percussion. Basically, an orchestra is a symphony if it is capable of playing symphonies. These are long pieces, usually of three or more movements, written for orchestras with full percussion sections, piano, harp, bassoons, oboes, an organ, a special guy to play the triangle, etc. For instance, Beethoven's Symphony No. 9 (known as the "Choral Symphony" and containing the famous "Ode to Joy") calls for the following instruments: flute, oboe, clarinet, bassoon, French horn, trumpet, timpani, violin I and violin II, viola, cello, bass viol, full chorus, and solo soprano, alto, tenor, and bass vocalists. In the modern era, composers have gone farther and farther afield to bring unique sounds to their symphonies, including everything from trash cans and kazoos to typewriters and washing machines. So when does a symphony become a philharmonic? Basically, if there's another symphony already in town. These days, the term "philharmonic" is mostly used to distinguish a symphony orchestra from another symphony orchestra in the same city. Vienna, for instance, has the Vienna Symphony Orchestra and the Vienna Philharmonic Orchestra. The word *philharmonic* means nothing more than "harmony-loving."

Now with Authentic Intestines

A recent trend in symphonies has been to try to recreate what musical pieces sounded like when they were first performed on authentic period instruments, including violins strung with catgut (don't worry, it's not really cat—it's actually sheep intestine).

o o o o o o o o o o o

Ella Fitzgerald vs. Billie Holiday

The Dilemma: You know they sing jazz. You know they're important. But that's where your knowledge stops.

People You Can Impress: anybody smart enough to know great jazz when they hear it

The Quick Trick: If there's a white gardenia in her hair, that's Billie Holiday. If you hear some scat singing, it's probably Ella.

The Explanation:

These immortal jazz divas are often considered two sides of the same coin. On one hand, you've got Ella: the revered grand dame of her art, with a long list of recordings and accomplishments. On the other, there's Billie, the quintessential troubled artist. Billie wasn't just taken away too soon—she also squandered her gifts in a heartbreaking spiral of self-destruction.

But back to Ella. Born in 1917, Fitzgerald was known as much for her incredible musicianship as she was for her unbelievable voice. Journalist David Brinkley, once commenting on her impressive three-octave vocal range, said you'd need an elevator to get from bottom to top. But while range is one thing, what you do with it is quite another. And the "First Lady of Song" did like no other. Using her voice like a trumpet, Ella produced a sound that was full, strong, rich, and flexible. Further, she was famous for her scat singing (you know, the "be-do-nde-be-doo-BAP!" stuff jazz some singers do), through which she could use her voice just like any other improvisational instrument in the band.

It's no wonder that Ella earned the awe and admiration of the biggest musical stars of the jazz era and beyond, including Duke Ellington, Count Basie, Louis Armstrong, George and Ira Gershwin, and Charlie Parker. Her reputation and respect were such that other musicians simply called her Lady Ella. And over her astonishing career, she recorded almost 70 albums and won 13 Grammys. Unfortunately, Ella lost her sight and eventually her legs to diabetes. And the world lost *her* in 1996.

Billie Holiday, on the other hand, led a life that was much shorter, but no less important in the history of jazz. Born Eleanora Fagan, Billie was child to a 13-year-old mother in Philadelphia. A dropout and a teenage prostitute, Billie's life started to change when she was discovered in a Harlem nightclub at age 17. And though she didn't have nearly the range of Fitzgerald, Holiday made up for it in spades with her gut-wrenching emotion and nuance. Her voice, though thinner than Ella's, carries a looser and more elastic approach to the words and phrasing that makes her instantly recognizable. If you want to get chills up your spine, catch an earful of "Strange Fruit," a hauntingly sad yet eerily beautiful lament by Lewis Allen about widespread lynching in the South: "Black bodies swinging in the southern breeze, / Strange fruit hanging from the poplar trees." As for titles, however, Billie too was a "lady." Her stage persona was Lady Day, and you can always recognize her by the white gardenia in her hair.

o o o o o o o o o o

Monet vs. Manet

The Dilemma: To the untrained eye, Monet and Manet come across like the kids from *The Parent Trap*. They have similar names, both were French, they're both heavily associated with Impressionism, and worst of all, they were friends.

People You Can Impress: people who like arts and crafts

The Quick Trick: Take a step closer to the painting. If you're looking at tiny dabs of paint working together to create a landscape, chances are you've got a Monet in front of you. If, on the other hand, you're looking at loosely painted images of chubby Parisians, you're probably staring at a Manet.

The Explanation:

Édouard Manet (eh-DWAHR mah-NAY) laid the groundwork for Impressionism, while Claude Monet (clode moh-NAY) perfected it. Born eight years before his contemporary, Manet's use of broad, simple color areas and his vivid, quick brush technique influenced painters like Monet and Renoir to fully develop Impressionist style. While imbued with the belief that art should reflect the ideals of the present rather than the past, Manet refused to exhibit his work as an Impressionist. The style was considered revolutionary at the time, and Manet preferred the adulation of more conservative audiences. So he stuck to studio drawing, painting over his penciled sketches.

Claude Monet, on the other hand, was an out-of-the-closet Impressionist. He was obsessed with capturing the fleeting effects of light and color on nature. To get the moment down on paper, he realized he had to use quick brushstrokes filled with individualized color (no time for drawings—Monet needed immediate brush-on-canvas action!). While Monet's first Impressionist works were met with plenty of criticism and contempt, he continued to paint in the style throughout his long life. Monet and Manet were great friends and admirers of each other's work. Manet used to help out the thin-walleted Monet with cash in his younger years, while Monet spurred a public effort to buy Manet's *Olympia* for the French nation, believing (correctly, as it turned out) it would become one of the most important works of the time.

Name-Dropping

Paintings to know (and mention) by each artist:

Monet: *Impression: Sunrise, The Water Lily Pond,* and *Houses of Parliament*

Manet: *Olympia, The Absinthe Drinker,* and *Luncheon on the Grass*

o o o o o o o o o o o

Art Deco vs. Art Nouveau

The Dilemma: You don't want to look like an idiot on *Antiques Roadshow.*

People You Can Impress: architecture buffs, art collectors, absinthe addicts, and flappers

The Quick Trick: It all comes down to "flowery" vs. "streamlined." Art Nouveau is the decorative one. Art Deco is sleeker.

The Explanation:

Both the Art Nouveau and Art Deco movements emerged as reactions to major world events; the Industrial Revolution and World War I, respectively. While both embraced modernist elements, they're easy to distinguish if you know what to look for.

Art Nouveau (it means "new art," but you probably figured that out) reigned from roughly 1880 until just before World War I. Art Nouveau embraced Europe's new industrial aesthetic rather than challenging it. It features naturalistic but stylized forms, often combined with more geometric shapes, particularly arcs, parabolas, and semicircles (think of the paintings of Gustav Klimt, or the arches of the Eiffel Tower). The movement brought in natural forms that had often been overlooked, like insects, weeds, even mythical faeries, as evidenced by Lalique jewelry or Tiffany lamps. The black and gold robe Kate Winslet doffs in the erotic portrait session scene in *Titanic* is quintessentially Art Nouveau.

Art Deco, on the other hand, emerged after World War I. In fact, the deprivations of the Great War years gave way to a whole new opulence and extravagance that defined the Jazz Age and the Art Deco aesthetic. The movement, prevalent from the 1920s until roughly the start of World War II, took it's name from the 1925 Exposition Internationale des Arts Décoratifs et Industriels Modernes (say that ten times, fast), held in France and is characterized by streamlined and geometric shapes. It also utilized modern materials like chrome, stainless steel, and inlaied wood. If Art Deco dabbled with natural materials, they tended to be graphic or textural, like zebra skin or jagged fern leaves. As a result, Deco featured bold shapes like sunbursts and zigzags and broad curves. In fact, if you check out the spire of the Chrysler Building, the hotels of Miami's South Beach, or the "coffin nose" of a 1935 Cord Model 810, you'll be staring at the very definition of Deco.

Of course, you don't *have* to go outdoors if you're looking for Deco. Furniture from the period—like the black leather and chrome chaise longue by Le Corbusier or the Barcelona chair by Bauhaus giant Ludwig Mies van der Rohe—is still coveted by design aficionados and can be found in finer hotel lobbies everywhere.

o o o o o o o o o o

Impressionism vs. Expressionism

The Dilemma: You've just sidled up to someone very attractive at an art museum. She asks you if you like the Impressionists. You think she means Darryl Hammond.

People You Can Impress: art collectors, fans of water lilies, ghostly guys screaming on bridges

The Quick Trick: If it looks like something recognizable but not too detailed, it's Impressionism. If it doesn't look like much of anything, it's Expressionism. If it *really* doesn't look like anything, it's *Abstract* Expressionism.

The Explanation:

Fact is there is no such thing as a cut-and-dried art movement. For the most part, the labels we give 'em just represent the trends that influence artists at a particular time. Which means movements are basically fluid and they always overlap. But knowing that, take a look at a few broad "strokes" to be aware of.

Impressionism arose around the mid-19th century as painters began to realize that they no longer needed to represent reality in stark detail; after all, photography had taken care of that. Instead they began painting their subjects more vaguely, with more emphasis on light and feeling than on detail—in short, capturing the *impression* the subject made on artist and viewer. For the most part, they used thickly textured paint to connote movement and a spirit of spontaneity. Despite the fact that Impressionism was in part a reaction to photography, it also ended up borrowing from the medium, mainly mimicking photography's composition, motion, and candor. Frequently working outdoors, Impressionists often painted the same subject in different lights (Monet's series of Venice, for example). Interestingly enough, "impressionism" was originally used as a pejorative. But artists quickly hijacked the intended insult and wore it proudly. Naturally, the Impressionists were followed by the Postimpressionists, who weren't so much copycats as artists that pushed the limits even farther, taking greater and greater license with conventional representation. Giants of Postimpressionism include Seurat, Cézanne, Toulouse-Lautrec, Gauguin, and a fella named Van Gogh.

About the only things Impressionism and Expressionism have in common is that they both included paint and they kind of rhyme. While Impressionism was all about the effect of the subject on the viewer, Expressionism was the artist *expressing* his or her own interior. It arose in the late 19th and early 20th centuries, and brought us artists like Wassily Kandinsky and Edvard Munch, whose works convey raw feelings, angst, or movement. It also gave us writers like Franz Kafka and composers like Arnold Schoenberg. As for blurring the lines, some regard Van Gogh as a proto-Expressionist because of his enormous influence on the movement.

Keeping It Abstract

As for America's modern contribution to the arts, it didn't arrive until after World War II, with Abstract Expressionism. It's *abstract* because the art was about pure feeling and less about representing the subject, if there even was one.

o o o o o o o o o o o

Ionic vs. Doric vs. Corinthian Columns

The Dilemma: You wouldn't know an Ionic entablature if it bit you on your portico.

People You Can Impress: snooty neighbors with big columns on their porches

The Quick Trick: The more syllables, the more ornate: Dor-ic, I-on-ic, Cor-in-thi-an.

The Explanation:

Although invented by the ancient Greeks, these three architectural orders are still very much alive thanks to the popular Greek Revival styles of government buildings, churches, and museums.

To begin with, the three names refer to orders, or overall styles, but their most recognizable distinctions are in their columns. The simplest and earliest style is the Doric (seventh to fifth centuries BCE). Doric columns have no base, the shafts are usually fluted (or grooved), and they're topped with simple, flared capitals. On top of that lies a square slab known as the abacus. The columns also support the entablature (containing the frieze), which in turn supports the triangular pediment (or basically, the roof). All that's to say that these features are all pretty plain in the Doric order, and any ornamentation is generally simple and understated. For a (mostly) Doric example, check out the Parthenon.

Next in chronology and complexity comes the Ionic order, arising in the sixth century BCE in Greek Ionia. You can't miss Ionic columns: They have scrolls (or, to be fancy, volutes) at the top and simple bases at the bottom. The tablature is more decorative, including bas-relief carvings of historical events or myths on the frieze. Next time you're at the Acropolis, note the Erechtheum (it's not what it sounds like). It's as Ionic as they come.

That brings us to Corinthian (fourth century BCE and later), an order used more in classical revivals than it ever was in classical architecture. Corinthian is the fanciest of the three, and there's only one word you need to know: leaves. Intricately carved, the leaves and rosettes of Corinthian capitals are said to have been developed by the architect Callimachus and were inspired by an acanthus plant he saw growing through a woven basket on a grave. The base is multilayered, the abacus is concave on each side, and the entablature is divided into many more highly ornamented layers. To see the height of Corinthian-ness, go to D.C. The U.S. Capitol building has more Corinthian columns than it knows what to do with.

Extra Credit

Italian Renaissance architects recognized two additional orders: the Tuscan, a style even plainer than Doric, with unfluted columns and unadorned entablatures, common in Georgian architecture; and the Composite, a ridiculously ornamented style that combined Corinthian leaves, Ionic volutes, and anything else you wanted to throw in there.

Marvel vs. DC

The Dilemma: After being rescued from a supervillain's lair by a guy in tights, you offer to pay for his dry cleaning. So who do you make the check out to, DC Comics or Marvel Comics?

People You Can Impress: geeks, nerds, Sons of Krypton, and teenagers bitten by radioactive spiders

The Quick Trick: Marvel's biggest names—Spider-Man, The X-Men, The Hulk, Fantastic Four. DC's biggest names—Batman, Superman, Justice League of America, Wonder Woman.

The Explanation:

The Marvel vs. DC dogfight has raged since the beginning of comic book time. DC is older, taking its name from 1937's *Detective Comics*. In June 1938, the company released what would become the most valuable comic ever: *Action Comics* #1, introducing a fella from Krypton called Superman. This essentially launched the Golden Age of comics, in which DC introduced icons like Bob Kane's Batman (in the also ridiculously valuable *Detective Comics* #27, 1939), The Flash, Hawkman, and The Green Lantern (all in 1940), Aquaman (in 1941), and Wonder Woman (in 1942).

Meanwhile, the company's rival, Timely Comics, staked its claim with *Marvel Comics* #1 in 1939, introducing future mainstays the Human Torch and the Sub-Mariner. A new hero, Captain America, debuted the next year when the legendary writer Joe Simon and incredible artist Jack Kirby combined powers.

After waning through the '40s and '50s, the costumed hero genre rose again in the late '50s with DC's *Justice League of America*. In 1962 Timely, now called Marvel Comics, introduced the Fantastic Four, the brainchild of Kirby and a writer pen-named Stan Lee. The Silver Age had begun, and it would introduce the biggest hero of the era: Spider-Man. The creation of Lee (who would later go on to lead Marvel) and artist Steve Ditko, Spider-Man debuted in 1962's *Amazing Fantasy* #15.

As for differences, one big distinction between the companies is characterization and setting. Marvel gets credit from fans for making heroes out of more realistic characters (think of the teen misfit Peter Parker as Spider-Man, or Logan, the angry, dangerous alter ego of Wolverine) who live in real places, like New York City. DC fans counter with the dark, tormented persona of Batman's Bruce Wayne, although DC has often based its action in fictional places like Gotham, Metropolis, and Smallville.

In the 1970s, Marvel attempted to buy DC and all its characters. In true comic fashion, DC screamed "*Never!*" and sold to Warner Communications instead. Since then, Warner has revived DC franchises with the huge Batman movies and Superman TV shows *Lois and Clark* and *Smallville*. Graphic novels from DC and its subsidiary imprints have also been hugely successful, like *The Watchmen* and *The Sandman* series, or made into movies, including *From Hell* and *The League of Extraordinary Gentlemen*. Marvel, too, has continued to roll with the success of its Spider-Man, The X-Men, The Hulk, and Fantastic Four franchises.

○ ○ ○ ○ ○ ○ ○ ○ ○ ○

Pyramid vs. Ziggurat

The Dilemma: You're a god-king and you'd like to get a little closer to your fellow deities. So should your 20,000 slaves build you a pyramid or a ziggurat?

People You Can Impress: archaeologists, Egyptologists, the gods

The Quick Trick: South America and Egypt built pyramids. Mesopotamia built ziggurats, which look like South American pyramids with ramps.

The Explanation:

We'll start with the most famous, the Egyptian pyramids. Today it's generally believed these towering structures were tombs. What has been found inside, however, is precisely executed layouts. For example, inside each pyramid a narrow shaft extends from the innermost chamber to the outside, aligned exactly with the polestar. Thus archaeologists have argued that the pyramids were thought to be a vessel or machine to get the pharaohs to the heavens.

The pyramids are spooky for many reasons. The stones are laid so exactly that you can't even fit a knife blade between them. They're almost perfectly square, and aligned to the points of the compass with uncanny accuracy. And while there are pyramids at several spots in Egypt, the best known are at the Giza "Necropolis" (City of the Dead). Of course, the jewel of these structures is the Great Pyramid of Khufu, a pharaoh of the fourth dynasty who you may also know by his Greek name, Cheops. In fact, until the 14th century, the Great Pyramid was the world's tallest *building*.

A debate has long raged about how the darn things got built. The current leading theory is that a ramp spiraled up from the quarry and around the rising structure. The ton-and-a-half stone blocks were moved on wooden sleds most likely lubricated by water or, as some have suggested, milk. As impressive as the pyramids are today, picture them in their original form, covered with gleaming white blocks of smoothed limestone.

The pyramids of South America, no less impressive, have a stair-stepped design that reflects their different purpose. These structures were temples to the gods, and each was fronted by a massive staircase and topped with a temple. In the Aztec capital of Tenochtitlán (now Mexico City), for example, there was a huge pyramid called Templo Mayor where at one ritual in 1487, 20,000 people were supposedly sacrificed.

Egypt and South America don't have a monopoly on pyramids, however. There are 16 of them in Greece, some even older than those at Giza. China has 'em, too, as does Sudan.

Ziggurats are a lot like the South American pyramids, with their stair-stepped shape and temple tops. But ziggurats were not places of worship; to the Sumerians, Assyrians, and Babylonians that built them, they were the gods' actual homes. In fact, only priests could enter. And while South American pyramids have long staircases, ziggurats have ramps and steps. Many ziggurats also had seven tiers, representing the seven known planets or the seven heavens. For the most part, the ziggurats that still exist can be found mainly in Iran and Iraq.

o o o o o o o o o o

Romanesque vs. Gothic Architecture

The Dilemma: Both are styles of medieval architecture that you associate with churches—but that's all you've got.

People You Can Impress: Europeans (no mean feat for Yanks these days)

The Quick Trick: If it has flying buttresses, pointed arches, and rose windows, it's Gothic.

The Explanation:

You can't swing *un chat mort* in Europe without hitting a really old cathedral. And after your first three or four, they all start to look alike: stone, majestic, impossibly huge. But if they were built between 800 and 1500, there's a darn good chance they fall into one of these categories.

Prevalent from the ninth through 12th centuries CE, Romanesque architecture combined the influences of Roman and Byzantine styles. In fact, the architecture got its name (in the 1800s, by the way) because one of its key features, the barrel vault, bore such a resemblance to the classical Roman arch. At the time, religious pilgrims were traveling to various shrines throughout Europe, creating the need for buildings much larger than the traditional basilica-style churches. The use of barrel vaults thus allowed for huge interior spaces built entirely of stone. But that also meant the roofs were extremely heavy, so the walls had to be tremendously thick to prevent buckling. Strong walls also meant fewer windows, so the insides of Romanesque churches often look dim and feel like fortresses.

As for Gothic architecture, although the word is now primarily associated with excessive eyeliner and trench coats, the style was born in the mid-12th century with the intention of making churches look like heaven: soaring, colorful, and bright. The biggest difference in Gothic style was the use of flying buttresses. These support structures or towers, set off from the main walls and attached by arches, displaced the pressure from the roof outward. Essentially, this meant the buildings could get taller, walls could get thinner, and there could be a *lot* of stained-glass windows. Gothic churches sport huge, ornate, petaled round masterpieces called rose windows. Further, Gothic cathedrals were also much pointier than their predecessors, with pointed arches and tall spires (instead of blunt towers) characterizing the style.

Name-Dropping

Buildings to mention when discussing the Romanesque and Gothic styles:

Romanesque: the Cathedral of Pisa (which includes the Leaning Tower), Italy; France's Mont St. Michel.

Gothic: Westminster Abbey, London; the Abbey of St. Denis and Notre Dame Cathedral, both in Paris; St. Peter's in Rome (a Renaissance example); and Chartres Cathedral in France

o o o o o o o o o o

Jogging vs. Racewalking

The Dilemma: That smug show-off at the gym is definitely doing *something* when he laps you—you're just not sure what it is.

People You Can Impress: track nerds and, well, more track nerds?

The Quick Trick: Check out the feet. The rules of racewalking are specific about what should be happening down there. No matter how fast you're going, as long as at least one of your feet is always touching the ground, and as long as you're not bending your knees, you're racewalking.

The Explanation:

With roughly 400 years of history under their collective belt (or fanny pack, as the case may be), racewalking enthusiasts have had plenty of time to pin down exactly what their sport entails. The whole thing began when (apparently bored) English nobles started holding races between their footmen, wagering on whose servant was the fastest. By the 19th century, racewalking was the second-biggest betting sport in America behind horse racing, and in 1908 it became an Olympic event. These days, the true champions of the sport can walk a mile in less than six minutes.

Jogging, on the other hand, has a much shorter history. It began as a conditioning activity for retired runners and gained popularity in America with the 1967 publication of *Jogging,* cowritten by University of Oregon track coach Bill Bowerman and cardiologist Dr. Waldo Harris. Only then did average Americans begin regularly participating in "light running" as a way to stay in shape.

○ ○ ○ ○ ○ ○ ○ ○ ○ ○

Billiards vs. Pool vs. Snooker

The Dilemma: Not knowing what game you just played is Dilemma #1. Not knowing how to tell your wife you just lost the house? That's a tad trickier.

People You Can Impress: guys named after cities

The Quick Trick: Look at the table: If it's bigger than the standard American pool table, you're playing billiards or snooker. If there are more than three balls on this big table, it's definitely snooker.

The Explanation:

When it comes to distinguishing pool from other billiards games, size—and we're talking about tables here—definitely matters. Pool, for instance, is the game you'll probably find in most American bars, using tables that are generally 4½' × 9' (although tables can be as short as 7'). Billiards and snooker, on the other hand, are played on a huge table 6' × 12'.

Of course, there are other differences as well. The most common pool games are 8-ball and 9-ball. In 8-ball, a player must pocket all the balls of his type (stripes or solids) before sinking the eight ball. Nine-ball, however, only uses the balls numbered 1 through 9. And while the balls can be sunk in any order, the first ball *struck* every time must be the lowest-numbered one on the table. The first player to sink the 9-ball, even if other balls are still on the table, wins.

As for billiards and snooker, the first (semantic) rule of thumb is that balls are "potted," not "pocketed." English billiards uses only three balls: two cue balls and a red object ball. Billiards players can accumulate points in three ways: winners (potting the red ball), losers (potting your cue ball off the red ball), and canons (hitting the red ball and the opponent's cue ball in one stroke). If you're looking to rack up points, try combining these shots. Just like everything British, there are lots of rules—not to mention variations (including some that don't involve potting balls!). Generally, however, players alternate turns when one fails to pot a ball or fouls, and play continues until one of the players reaches a predetermined score.

Snooker, on the other hand, is a British obsession invented by Neville Chamberlain (he of appeasing Hitler fame). It uses 22 balls: 15 red; one each of yellow, green, brown, blue, pink, and black; and a cue ball. It too has lots of rules, but the basic object is to alternately sink red balls and colored balls. Each red is worth one point, and the others range from two points for the yellow up to seven for the black. Oh, and red balls stay in the pockets and colored balls keep coming back out until all the reds are gone. Then the game finishes with everyone trying to sink the colors in the correct order. Whatever individual or team has the most points wins. Whew! And you thought calculus was hard.

Good to Know

According to the Billiard Congress of America, during the Civil War billiard results often received wider coverage than war news.

○ ○ ○ ○ ○ ○ ○ ○ ○ ○

Foil vs. Épée vs. Saber

The Dilemma: You've got to defend your honor, you're just not exactly sure how.
Materials Needed: a tolerance for French words
People You Can Impress: your aforementioned mortal enemy, Zorro, and fans of *The Princess Bride*

The Explanation:

To the uninitiated, fencing can be a bit baffling. For instance, in modern fencing, the touches are registered electronically but there's still a referee (also called a president) who can call hits that didn't register electronically or overrule ones that did. But all that's beside the point. To begin with, fencing can be broken down into three major categories.

The first is foil, the lightest and most flexible of the fencing weapons. In foil, the only valid target is the opponent's trunk (roughly from the top of the collar to the crotch in front, and to the top of the hipbones in the back). The arms, legs, and head are no good, and only hits with the foil's tip are counted. Basically, foil fencing is a modernized form of what was, traditionally, sword-fighting practice—like, if someone made a sport out of hitting tackling blocks.

If you are really dueling with a seriously sharp rapier, any touch anywhere on the body would smart. And that's the origin of the épée, a heavier, more rigid version of the foil, with a triangular blade and a larger, "bowl-shaped" blade guard (to protect the hand). In épée, a person's whole body is fair game, including the head. Like foil, épée touches must be made with only the tip, and both disciplines require the fencers to stop after each touch is made, whether on a valid target area or not.

The last discipline is saber, an incredibly fast-paced whack fest that's a hand-me-down from the days of cavalrymen slashing away on horseback. The fencing saber is heavier and has a large, curved hand guard. The target area is anything from the waist up (the parts you'd be swinging at if you and your opponents were both on horses). But two big differences make saber the most frenetic of the disciplines. First, the edge of the saber can be used as well as the point, so slashes are valid hits; and second, the bout does not stop after an off-target hit, so the opponents will whack and slash at each other until a legal hit is registered, making it a hoot to watch.

Vocab Lesson

Like ballet, fencing is of (mostly) French origin and uses a list of French words longer than the average *baguette*. For instance, the strip on which the bouts take place is the *piste*. An attack that strongly grazes the opponent's blade is a *froissement*. One that starts before a stoppage in play but lands after is called a *coup lancé*. And a leaping, running attack is called a *flèche*.

o o o o o o o o o o

Yoga vs. Pilates

The Dilemma: You want to exercise, but you prefer something that chills you out instead of buffing you up. Should you take yoga or Pilates?

People You Can Impress: Indian guys with incredibly long beards or instructors with incredibly developed core muscles

The Quick Trick: There is no quick trick to exercise. It takes commitment!

The Explanation:

We in the western hemisphere tend to think of yoga as a way to stretch out or shed stress. But the practice began as something very spiritual. Those who practiced yoga (yogis) did so to control their bodies and free themselves from temptation and achieve nirvana. In fact, yoga actually predates Hinduism.

The main yoga practiced outside India today is called hatha yoga. The point is to balance your body and your mind through controlled breathing (*pranayama*), mental focus, and a series of postures called asanas, like the well-known Lotus (*padmasana*) and Downward-Facing Dog (*adho mukha svanasana*). Some ascribe a spiritual dimension to the practice akin to its Eastern origins. This kundalini yoga uses asanas to release life energy clustered in seven chakras, or centers of spiritual energy.

Bikram, a kind of "hot yoga" named after its originator, increases flexibility (and sweating) by doing yoga in a really hot room. Bikram, by the way, is not quite as exotic as it sounds: The main studio is on La Cienega Boulevard in L.A.

Pilates, on the other hand, combines the idea of mind-and-body union with an emphasis on physical development and fitness. It was originally named Contrology by its inventor, Joseph H. Pilates, and although it's not as old as yoga, it's older than you'd think. Pilates came up with the exercises while working as a nurse during World War I! His focus was to "control" the muscles with the consciousness. Instead of lots of repetitions of simple movements (like dumbbell curls), Pilates stressed doing fewer reps of more skilled movements, thereby engaging the mind. He came up with over 500 of these (today there are thousands). Of course, his original method involved a lot of specially designed machines as well (basically modified gymnastics apparatuses, with springs added for resistance), including the Spine Corrector Barrel and the Cadillac, the latter involving a bench and parallel bars and looking an awful lot like a torture device.

The Pilates method gained popularity in the U.S. when it was espoused by two dance giants of the era: Martha Graham and George Balanchine. Along with yoga, it saw a huge resurgence in the 1990s, when it was heavily endorsed by Madonna.

Celebrity Roundup

Every celebrity faces a stark choice during his or her ride on the fame train: Will I choose yoga or Pilates?

Yoga: Ricky Martin, Meg Ryan, Jerry Seinfeld, Kareem Abdul-Jabbar, Jamie Lee Curtis, and Gwyneth Paltrow

Pilates: Jennifer Aniston, Lucy "Xena" Lawless, Hugh Grant, Patrick Swayze, Daisy Fuentes, and Rod Stewart

o o o o o o o o o o o

Canadian Football vs. Australian Rules

The Dilemma: Three football players—an American, a Canadian, and an Aussie—walk into a bar. Who has the worst limp?

People You Can Impress: manly sports enthusiasts in former British colonies

The Quick Trick: If the players don't have padding, it's Australian for football.

The Explanation:

Rather than rip off American football, the Canadian Football League actually started as modified English rugby, then borrowed heavily from its American counterpart until the two were almost identical. The first difference you'll notice about Canadian football is the field. It's *huge*—110 yards long (with two 50 yard lines and a center line), 65 yards wide, with end zones 20 yards deep.

Canadian play is similar to American football, with interesting differences. There are 12 players to a side. The game moves fast, as the play clock is only 20 seconds and you have to go ten yards in only *three* downs. The backfield can have unlimited motion before the snap, so you can have receivers and "slot backs" moving at once, even toward the line of scrimmage (so they can be at a full run when the ball is snapped). There's an added way to score, too. On a kickoff, punt, or—get this—*missed field goal,* the receiving team must advance the ball out of the end zone or the kicking team gets a point (called a single, or rouge).

Today the CFL is composed of nine teams, including the Montréal Alouettes ("The Als") and the Edmonton Eskimos, with the perennial powerhouse (or power*hoos* if you're Canadian) being the Toronto Argonauts. They've won the coveted Grey Cup (their Super Bowl) 14 times.

Australian Rules Football ("Aussie Rules" or, more charmingly, "Footy") is what happens when a penal colony decides to play rugby. The huge field is a modified cricket oval, but there's no standard size. You've got a center square, two 50-meter arcs, two 10-meter goal squares, and four posts at each end (two very tall goal posts flanked by shorter "behind posts"). Each side gets 18 players, with cool positions like ruckman, rover, ruck rover, half-forward, and back pocket.

Play starts with a "centre bounce" (or "ball up") and the ruckmen jump for it. The ball is bigger and rounder than an American football. You can kick or punch the ball but not throw it. You can also run as far as you want with it, but you have to bounce it every 15 meters. If you're tackled, you must kick or punch the ball away to a teammate. If you catch a kicked ball cleanly, that's called a mark, and you get a free kick toward the other team's goal. Kick the ball between the two center posts for a goal (six points), or between one of the center poles and a behind pole for a "behind" (one point). As for scoring, you can tell who just scored what by watching umpires in white lab coats and funny hats make appropriate pointy motions.

The sport is one of constant motion and an absolute blast to watch. The tackling is truly brutal, and acrobatic "high marks" or "species" are spectacular. Plus, they don't wear pads. Heck, their "guernseys" don't even have *sleeves.*

Baseball vs. Cricket

The Dilemma: You've heard watching both these games feels like an eternity. But which mind-numbing sport is the right one for you?

People You Can Impress: Mystified fans of either sport who don't understand the other.

The Quick Trick: Is the bat round? You're watching baseball. Is it flat? Then it's cricket. (A slightly slower trick would be to hang around for five days. If the game's still going on, it's cricket!)

The Explanation:

The technical aspects of these games are very different. Baseball has nine players, cricket has eleven; cricket has two bases, whereas baseball has four. But their foremost difference is philosophical. In short, baseball favors defense, while cricket favors offense. Consider the 2003 baseball season in which the prolific Boston Red Sox scored 961 runs in a 162-game season. By comparison, the average cricket team scores 320 runs in a *single* match. There is also a faster rotation of players in baseball. A rotation of nine batters will have their chance at the plate, or be "put out," four or five times in a game. In cricket, however, it takes about six hours to retire (or call out) eight men.

A cricket batsman can be retired in one of three ways: The bowler (pitcher) can knock over the offense's wickets—a set of sticks set up behind the batsmen; a field player can catch a battled ball before it bounces; or a fielder may tag the base the batter is trying to reach before he gets there. It sounds easy, but it isn't. In fact, since a cricketer bats until he's retired, it's not uncommon for a batsman to drive in 50 to 100 runs in a single turn. (Can you imagine Barry Bonds hitting a homer, trotting around the bases, and then picking up the bat to hit again, and again, and again?)

So why are these cricket batsmen so hard to call out? Number one, they never have to swing. In baseball, if you let pitch after pitch go by, you'll either walk or be struck out, ending your time at the plate. But in cricket, you can swing whenever the mood strikes. Plus, even when a cricketer does make contact, he's not required to run. If he doesn't like his chances of making it safely to the other base, he can just stay there and try again. Other cricketer advantages include the ability to hit the ball in any direction (no foul lines here) and a hefty 6-run score for batting the ball over the fence. *Six runs?* That means Barry Bonds's record-setting 73 single-season homers would have been worth 438 runs. Wow. Then he wouldn't even have needed steroids (allegedly).

o o o o o o o o o o

Tag vs. Kabaddi

The Dilemma: Everyone's running around in total chaos (and you kind of want to join in).

People You Can Impress: Anyone who knows what kabbadi is.

The Quick Trick: Are the players over 10 years old? Congrats, you're watching kabaddi (we hope!)

The Explanation:

Tag is a simple child's game. Kabaddi is a simple child's game taken to maddening heights of silliness. To clarify "tag," we're talking about freeze tag, blob tag, "you're it" tag, team tag, and any other of the variations of the game where the object is to touch another person, thereby rendering him or her "out" or "it."

To clarify "kabaddi," we mean breath-holding, scary, chanting tag. Enjoyed primarily in India, kabaddi is a team sport played on a bisected field about the size of a volleyball court. Each team consists of twelve players, with seven of them taking the court at a time. The teams alternate offense and defense. The offensive team designates a "raider"—a player chosen to infiltrate enemy territory and "tag" as many opposing players as he can. The tricky bit? He's only allowed one breath's time to do all his tagging. To prove that he hasn't drawn another breath, the raider is required to chant the name of the sport the entire time he's on enemy soil. "Kabaddikabaddikabaddikabaddikabaddi . . ." If he can't get back to his team's side before stopping his chant, he's out. Strangestrangestrangestrangestrange. . . .

Good to Know

While you probably won't need a translation service to join in a foreign game of tag, you just never know (kids can be so cruel). So, in an effort to make sure words don't provide any sort of stumbling block, we've provided a handy translation guide to help you out.

In:	**Tag is sometimes called:**
Japan	Onigokko (where "It" is called "Oni")
England	It, dobby, tic, or tig
Ireland	Chasing
Brazil	Pega Pega ("catch catch")
Australia	Tiggy, tips, or chasey
Finland	Hippa
Colombia	La Lleva ("the carrying")
France	Chat ("cat")

Not So Different After All

o o o o o o o o o o

P. DIDDY AND GANDHI

Gandhi: Bald

P. Diddy: Sometimes shaves his head

Gandhi: Made his own clothes

P. Diddy: Has his own clothing line, Sean John

Gandhi: Sometimes arrested for civil disobedience

P. Diddy: Sometimes arrested

Gandhi: Famously ascetic

P. Diddy: Kind of athletic

Gandhi: Afraid of the dark (he always slept with a lamp burning by his bedside.)

P. Diddy: Also afraid of the dark (when the electricity went out during a post-MTV Europe Music Awards show party held at the Mirabe Club in Barcelona in 2002, he threw a temper tantrum and then hightailed it to a hotel.)

o o o o o o o o o o

CHURCHILL AND MAE WEST

Winston: Dropped bombshells

Mae West: Was a bombshell

Winston: Brunette (before he went bald)

Mae West: Brunette (before she dyed her hair)

Winston: Admired horses ("There is something about the outside of a horse that is good for the inside of a man.")

Mae West: Once guest-starred on *Mr. Ed.*

Winston: Favored dry martinis (his recipe: "Glance at the vermouth bottle briefly while pouring the juniper distillate freely.")

Mae West: Favored dry martinis ("Let's get out of these wet clothes and into a dry martini.")

Groundhog vs. Woodchuck

THEY'RE THE SAME!

Both are names for *Marmota monax*, the pudgy herbivore. Ergo, February 2 is Woodchuck Day, and even the most tongue-tied among us can finally ask that age-old question: "How much wood would a groundhog chuck if a groundhog could chuck wood?"

o o o o o o o o o o

ALBERT EINSTEIN AND BEN FRANKLIN

Franklin: Genius

Einstein: Genius

Franklin: Famously flew a kite in a lightning storm

Einstein: Hairstyle famously looked like he'd flown a kite in a lightning storm

Franklin: Cheated on his first wife and fathered an illegitimate child

Einstein: Cheated on his first wife (with his own first cousin!) and fathered an illegitimate child

Franklin: Got involved in politics as an old man (after spending most of his life writing, working in printing, Franklin became a pivotal voice in the 1787 Constitutional Convention.)

Einstein: Almost got involved in politics as an old man (in 1952, Einstein was offered the presidency of Israel. He declined.)

o o o o o o o o o o

WHOOPI GOLDBERG AND JANE AUSTEN

Jane: Preacher's kid

Whoopi: Preacher's kid

Jane: Published anonymously (19th-century female authors usually did—or chose male pen names)

Whoopi: Works pseudonymously (birth name: Caryn Elaine Johnson)

Jane: Had a book named *Emma*

Whoopi: Had a mother named Emma

Jane: Author (of six novels, published between 1811 and 1818, all of which are considered classics)

Whoopi: Author (of the quasi-memoir *Book* and the children's picture book *Alice*, both of which are considered—well, not classics, certainly)

Mountain Lion vs. Cougar

THEY'RE THE SAME!

There are almost as many names for the cougar as there are actual cougars remaining in the world. Also known as pumas, catamounts, or panthers, the severely endangered cat, which lives only in North and South America, comes in several subspecies, but all its many nicknames refer to *Puma concolor.*

o o o o o o o o o o

CHEVY CHASE AND HELEN HUNT

Chevy: Was once the best-paid former *Saturday Night Live* cast member, earning $7 million a movie

Helen: Was once the best-paid actress in TV history, earning $1 million an episode for *Mad About You*

Chevy: Campaigned for John Kerry in 2004

Helen: Campaigned for John Kerry in 2004

Chevy: Has an anger management problem (was banned for life from hosting *Saturday Night Live* in 1997 after verbally abusing coworkers; and once brawled with, of all people, Bill Murray)

Helen: Gets pretty mad a couple times during *As Good As It Gets*

Chevy: Named after a small town (in Maryland)

Helen: Named her daughter, Makena'lei, after a small town (in Hawaii)

o o o o o o o o o o

TRUMAN CAPOTE AND HARPER LEE

Harper: Grew up in the small town of Monroeville, Alabama

Truman: Grew up in the small town of Monroeville, Alabama

Harper: Rather effeminate

Truman: Rather effeminate

Harper: May have written *To Kill a Mockingbird*

Truman: Also may have written *To Kill a Mockingbird*—at least according to a persistent but probably false rumor

Harper: Never wrote another book after the success of her only novel

Truman: Never completed another book after the success of *In Cold Blood*

Spy vs. Spy

THEY'RE THE SAME! (WELL, SORTA.)

Spy vs Spy, the *MAD* magazine comic strip created by Cuban exile Antonio Prohias, has been a fixture in popular culture since 1961. So what's the difference between the spies? One wears black, the other white. Their personalities, bomb-making techniques, and evasive maneuvers, however, are absolutely interchangeable, and each spy wins (by killing his nemesis) about 50 percent of the time.

o o o o o o o o o o

ABRAHAM LINCOLN AND TWO-YEAR-OLDS

Lincoln: Had a "willful, impudent, childish" wife (to quote her biographer)

Two-Year-Olds: Are generally willful, impudent, and childish

Lincoln: Openly wept the first time he heard "The Battle Hymn of the Republic"

Two-Year-Olds: Openly weep for any old reason

Lincoln: Once said of do-nothing General George McClellan: "If McClellan is not using the army, I should like to borrow it for a while."

Two-Year-Olds: Also constantly want to take stuff away from you

Lincoln: Most famous speech, *The Gettysburg Address,* contained exactly 272 words

Two-Year-Olds: According to a Harvard University study, the average two-year-old has a vocabulary of exactly 272 words ("civil" and "war" not among them).

o o o o o o o o o o

CAMERON DIAZ AND JACK JOHNSON

Jack: Became first African-American heavyweight champion in 1908 when he delivered a technical knockout to Tommy Burns

Cameron: Is, technically, a knockout

Jack: Upended convention by dating white women (Jackson was imprisoned for two years on trumped-up charges of "white slavery.")

Cameron: Upended convention by dating a younger man (Justin Timberlake is nine years Diaz's junior.)

Jack: Reportedly hit harder than anyone in his era

Cameron: Landed some pretty good blows in *Charlie's Angels: Full Throttle*

Jack: Was an amateur race car driver (frequently arrested for speeding, he tried life as a professional race car driver but couldn't cut it. But he never stopped driving fast—and died in a car crash in 1946 at the age of 58.)

Cameron: Also an amateur race car driver (participated in the 1998 Celebrity Grand Prix, in which the likes of Jim Belushi and that woman from *JAG* raced in cars that could reach 130 miles per hour.)

Stuffing vs. Dressing

THEY'RE THE SAME!

It's *stuffing* in the North and *dressing* in Dixie. Some say that stuffing is stuffed inside the turkey, while dressing is baked separately—but that's hogwash. Stuffing and dressing can both be cooked either way, because they are both the exact same thing.

Holland vs. the Netherlands

THEY'RE THE SAME!

Some say that calling the Netherlands "Holland" is equivalent to calling the United Kingdom "England." Holland, they point out, is merely part of the Kingdom of the Netherlands (which includes, among other things, the Caribbean island of Aruba). But as far as we're concerned, and as far as most Dutch people are concerned, Holland is perfectly acceptable. After all, when the Dutch chant at soccer games, they're singing "Holland! Holland!" not "The Kingdom of the Netherlands including the Netherlands Antilles!"

Consumption vs. Tuberculosis

THEY'RE THE SAME!

Back in the 19th century, when *everybody* had it (all four Brontë sisters, Paul Gauguin, Frédéric Chopin, Simón Bolívar, John Calvin—the list goes on and on), the pulmonary bacterial infection now known as tuberculosis was called consumption. Why? Because it seemed to consume people from the inside out.

Bipolar Disorder vs. Manic Depression

THEY'RE THE SAME!

In the 1990s, psychologists started to abandon the phrase "manic depression," because it implied that people with the disease must frequently cycle between mania and depression. But some people with bipolar disorder suffer manic episodes and depressive episodes years, or even decades, apart.

Movies vs. Films

THEY'RE THE SAME!

The only difference is that pretentious film students say *film* while the rest of us say *movie*. Some would argue that it's technically incorrect to say film when referring to a movie shot on digital video—but even if you really, really love semantics (and as you've surely noted, we really, really do), that's just dumb.

Mary Westmacott vs. Agatha Christie

THEY'RE THE SAME!

Agatha Christie's mystery novels have sold over a billion copies in English alone, making her history's bestselling author in English if you don't count William Shakespeare or all the people who wrote the Bible. But Christie had a secret: She enjoyed writing melodramatic, grandly tragic romance novels. Between 1930 and 1956, she published six under the pseudonym Mary Westmacott.

About the Editors

WILL PEARSON and **MANGESH HATTIKUDUR** met as freshmen at Duke University and in their senior year parlayed their cafeteria conversations into the first issue of ***mental_floss*** magazine. Five years later, they're well on their way to creating a knowledge empire. In addition to the magazine, a board game, and a weekly CNN *Headline News* segment, the two have also collaborated on five ***mental_floss*** books. In their spare time, Will and Mangesh enjoy touring the country doing magic shows under the stage name Penn and Teller.

JOHN GREEN is the author of the award-winning novel *Looking for Alaska* (2005), which has been translated into eight languages and is being made into a film by Paramount Pictures. John also contributes commentary to NPR's *All Things Considered*. When he was 17, a friend accused him of not knowing the difference between something and Shinola. A humiliated John then had to ask what Shinola was. Ever since, he's been a passionate advocate for Difference Knowledge.

About the Contributors

MAGGIE KOERTH

Following her graduation from the University of Kansas and a panicky three-month stint as an unemployed citizen of the new economy, Maggie Koerth came on board as ***mental**_floss*'s assistant editor in August of 2004. Still happily employed today, she lives in Birmingham, Ala., with her husband, Chris Baker, and her bipartisan cats, Red and Blue.

CHRISTOPHER SMITH

Longtime ***mental**_floss* contributor Christopher Smith is an advertising creative director in Dallas, Tex., where he has done award-winning work for Motel 6, Chick-fil-A, and many others. He is also an improv comedian, public speaker, scotch collector, and *Jeopardy!* champion. A native of upstate New York and graduate of Penn State University, he lives in Dallas with his wife, Heather, and their three small children—daughter, Clara, and twin sons, Callum and Finnegan. This is his third book for ***mental**_floss*.

CHRIS CONNOLLY is a New York City–born writer who lives in San Diego, California, with his wife Joy, son Oliver, and their bulldog, Brooklyn. Chris writes about travel, food, and adventure for super-important publications like *The New York Times* and *Men's Health*. Subjects he's covered for ***mental**_floss* over the years include forgotten presidents, mind-controlling parasites, going over Niagara Falls in a barrel and how the invention of the bicycle indirectly lead to women's liberation. His first book, a juicy memoir about three years he spent living in the former Soviet Union will be published once someone pays him to write it. Chris has that rare combination of will, intellect, and passion that make a man great. He is awesome.

Exclusive offer for

MENTAL_FLOSS BOOK READERS!

If you liked this ***mental_floss*** book, you're going to love ***mental_floss*** magazine. Hip, quick, quirky, and fun, ***mental_floss*** is the perfect antidote to dull conversations. Jam-packed with fascinating facts, lucid explanations, and history's juiciest secrets, ***mental_floss*** uncovers everything from black holes to the Dead Sea Scrolls, and laces it with just enough wit to keep you grinning for weeks. So, go ahead and pick up a copy. And an hour later, when your kids are tugging at your pant legs and your spouse is burning dinner, and you're busy wondering just where the time went, you'll realize that ***mental_floss*** doesn't just make learning easy, it makes it addictive.

Save 50% off the cover price

of this wonderful magazine. Go to
www.mentalfloss.com/bookspecial
or complete and mail the form below.

Please enter my subscription to mental_floss magazine immediately!
__ **6 issues (1 year) $14.95**
__ **12 issues (2 years) $27.95**
(Canadian orders add $10 per year; payable in U.S. funds)

Name: ____________________
Address: ____________________ **Apt / Suite #:** _____
City: ____________________ **State:** _____ **Zip:** __________

___ Check enclosed
___ Please charge my Visa/MC
Card #:____________________**Exp:**_____

Signature: ____________________

Mail this form to:
mental_floss
P.O. Box 1940
Marion, OH 43306-1940

WBOOKS